DATE DUE

straydog

kathe koja

speak

An Imprint of Penguin Group (USA) Inc.

SPEAK

Published by Penguin Group

Penguin Group (USA) Inc., 345 Hudson Street, New York, New York 10014, U.S.A.

Penguin Books Ltd, 80 Strand, London WC2R ORL, England

Penguin Books Australia Ltd, 250 Camberwell Road,

Camberwell, Victoria 3124, Australia

Penguin Books Canada Ltd, 10 Alcorn Avenue, Toronto, Ontario, Canada M4V 3B2

Penguin Books (N.Z.) Ltd, 182-190 Wairau Road, Auckland 10, New Zealand

First published in the United States of America by Farrar, Straus and Giroux, 2002

Published by Speak, an imprint of Penguin Group (USA) Inc., 2004

3 5 7 9 10 8 6 4

LIBRARY OF CONGRESS CATALOGING-IN-PUBLICATION DATA

Koja, Kathe.

Straydog / Kathe Koja.

p. cm.

Summary: Rachel, a teenager with a healthy dose of both aptitude and attitude,
begins to feel at home volunteering at an animal shelter.

ISBN 0-14-240071-8 (pbk.)

[1. Dogs—Fiction. 2. Animal shelters—Fiction. 3. Human–animal relationships—
Fiction. 4. Creative writing—Fiction. 5. Individuality—Fiction.
6. High schools—Fiction. 7. Schools—Fiction.] I. Title: Stray dog. II. Title.

PZ7.K8296St 2004 [Fic]—dc22 2003059131

Printed in the United States of America

My thanks to Rick Lieder, Aaron Mustamaa, Frances Foster, and the staff of the Michigan Anti-Cruelty Society, for the right answers at the right times.

Special thanks to Chris Schelling.

To P.F. and Equinox
one day again

straydog

1

*R*achel. *Raychel. Raechel.* Black spider ink in a preppy-green notebook, my right arm aching on the slope of the desk. *Rachelle. RC.* No matter how I spell it, I'm still me, still here, still writing junk in a junky notebook for Advanced Language Arts which doesn't make a lot of sense if you look around the room: at Jon Truman, Courtney DiMartino, Chelsea Thayne—Chelsea *Thayne?* The only thing she's advanced at is being an idiot, especially to me.

But I don't care, about her or this class; or this school either. My mother thinks I should love school: *You're so smart, it all comes so easily for you.* Sure it does. Like school is just about grades. Or: *It's the happiest time of your life!* I hate it when adults say that, like my parents, or some of the teachers . . . Not Mrs. Cruzelle, though. This may be a dumb class, but there's nothing dumb about her.

"They say to write what you know," she tells us now; she has kind of a speech problem, a lisp, like *They thay.* Kids make fun of her; sometimes she hears, I know she does, but she never says anything. "But I think it's much more important to write what you *don't* know. Or what hurts you, or scares you, or makes you feel sad. That's what this paper is all about . . . Rachel?" Now she's by my desk, black hair, black jacket, little silver dog-shaped pin. "How's it coming? Going to have something for me today?"

Radical. Rebel. RAY-CHILL. "Yeah," I say, arm half across the notebook page; she knows I'm lying but, Mrs. Cruzelle style, doesn't call me on it, so I scribble out my fifty names and try to think of something real to write.

Across the aisle Chelsea puts her hand up, peach-colored nails and a fat class ring, her boyfriend's ring, this week's boyfriend anyway; how does she do it? *Why* does she do it? "Mrs. Cruzelle? How long does it have to be?"

"Well, as long as it takes, Chelsea."

"As long as what takes?"

"Have you told everything you need to tell?" Mrs. Cruzelle is so patient, I don't know how she doesn't go nuts. "When you've told everything you need to tell, everything the reader needs to know, then stop."

Chelsea frowns; Jon Truman, behind her, flicks her hair with his pencil and she gives him a smile, a big flirty magazine-cover smile, I bet she smiles the same way at her mirror. Scribbling over my scribbles, I try again: what hurts me, makes me feel sad . . . And now Chelsea's looking at me, at my paper and "How long's yours?" she whispers.

Yeah, right. Ignore me like I'm nothing, less than nothing, until you want an answer. So I do what I usually do, which is ignore *her*, keep working, trying to work but "How long?" she insists, like I'm supposed to help, *required* to help and "Do your

4

own paper," I say under my breath, not looking up as she makes a noise, a gritty little noise through her teeth, bitch; did she say that? One desk up, Courtney DiMartino laughs, a sharp snicker like broken glass, but I don't look up, stay hunched over my desk, fast spider-scrawl as I keep writing: about a dog I once saw at the shelter, a big chocolate Lab mashed into a little tiny cage, he couldn't even stand up but there were too many dogs and not enough cages, too many strays and not enough homes, you bet it hurts and "That's it," says Mrs. Cruzelle, "time's up. Hand it in as you leave," as the bell goes, pushing chairs and backpack thump and "It's not done," I say as I pause at her desk, last one out as usual. "I'll hand it in after lunch."

"I can take it as is," she says. "It's a rough draft, remember?"

"No, I want to finish," and I do, partly in Bio 2—which is third hour, Mr. Karpecky, when there's no lab to do he mostly just drones—and partly at lunch, me on the east steps since the weather's halfway warm, notebook on my knees, a Cappuccino Swirl and an apple I'm not eating. From here you can see the stand of elms and oaks by the student parking lot, really old trees, much older than the school or the houses behind them. They make me feel better sometimes, as if all the bad stuff is temporary, as if what really matters is going to last . . . People think I'm weird for eating on the steps. They think I'm weird for a lot of reasons: because I say what I think, because I am who I am. Which is why I don't have a million friends. Or any, really; not what I consider friends. To me a friend is someone you can share yourself with, your real self. And I'm not sharing myself with *anybody* at this place.

My mother's always nagging me about my crappy social life:

You should make an effort, call people, you need to get out—out of what? into what? Why should I trade who I am for who they want me to be? So they can pat me on the head and put me in the normal-girl box? I'd rather be alone. I'd rather be a wild dog than jammed in someone's cage.

After last hour, History, I stop by Mrs. Cruzelle's to drop off the paper—"A Dog's Life," I called it. She's busy with some kid, a freshman, he looks ten years old and very nervous, so I just leave it on her desk. Anyway I have to hurry. Today's a shelter day.

Here's the drill: as soon as you get in, turn on the fan and open the vent. Collect any fecal specimens, ugh, and put them in the specimen cups. Get the dogs out of the cages and into the runs. Disinfect the cages, put the dogs back in. Hose down the runs. Fill the food and water dishes, making sure to check the cages for "special diet" cards. Note who needs grooming, and what—nail trim, ear cleaning, flea bath, whatever. Start exercising, biggest dogs first or the most hyper, whichever works best on a given day. (There's a fenced yard right behind the shelter, about half an acre with a couple of extremely peed-on trees.) Give more water after exercise, but not too much too fast, bloat can kill a dog. Write down anything that seems important on the cage cards; tell Melissa if something seems really wrong, like straining, or throwing up, or if you think a dog's getting kennel cough. Wash the floor. Then wash your hands, because you've probably got dog poop or something gross on them. Check and see if anybody else needs help, like out in the storage shed, or stuffing envelopes, or whatever. They don't let me answer the phone or work the adoption desk; technically you're supposed to be eighteen to do that, and anyway my job is Care Specialist—that's what they call it on the volunteer form. Then, if everything's done and nobody needs help, go do what you—what I—really came here to do: just hang out with the dogs.

I'm an animal person, I mean I like all animals, but I have a real thing for dogs. There's something so . . . I don't know, so *clean* about them, the way they love you, the way they trust that whatever you do is right. You can talk to them, tell them anything, all the bad stuff that's inside, things you could never tell anyone else; maybe they don't understand, but they listen. I love dogs.

I can't have one, though. My mother has major allergies, pills, inhalers, the whole deal, she can't even wash my clothes when I've been at the shelter. When I was a kid I didn't really understand, I mean I didn't see how having a dog could make anyone sick, I thought my parents were just being arbitrarily mean to me. And I wanted a pet more than anything in the world.

So Brad—that's my father; I call him Brad the Dad—Brad got me a tankful of these expensive tropical fish, like an animal's an animal, right? Fins, fur, what's the difference? Of course I had no clue how to take care of them, tropical fish are complicated, so in a week or two they all died, and of course Brad said that proved I shouldn't have a pet because I wasn't responsible enough. See how he thinks?

So with no pet and no chance for one I'd go down the street to see the Kaisers' poodle, Sassy. The Kaisers were old, and kind of crabby; Sassy was kind of crabby too, an ancient white dog with crusty brown eyes, but I didn't care, she'd let me pet her any time I wanted and that was good enough for me. Naturally

Brad thought this was a weird idea, that instead I ought to be out playing Barbie or whatever with the neighborhood girls, I used to hear him complain to my mother: *Why doesn't she have any friends? Why doesn't she play with that girl across the street, that blond kid, what's her name?*

Cara? my mother would say, in that anxious way she has. *Oh, I don't know, I don't think Rachel likes her.* Likes her? She used to spit in people's milk at school. But that wasn't good enough for Brad: *Rachel doesn't like anything, from what I can see. You let her get too isolated, Elisha,* and on and on, as if I was all her fault. I'd just block him out—I still do—but it would really get to my mother. She'd keep giving me these little suggestions, like why didn't I invite this or that girl over, why didn't I join the soccer league or AfterSchool Arts or drop-in gym or whatever. I tried to tell her why this was a bad idea, but after a while I just gave up; it was like the ugly duckling explaining why he wasn't going swimming with all the other little ducks.

So after school, when the other kids were in sports or band or going somewhere to play, I'd go off on my own: to the Kaisers' to hang out with Sassy, or to the very back of our back yard, by the honeysuckle vines, to sit watching the squirrels and birds and writing stories about them in my notebook. I have about a hundred of those notebooks, all piled in the back of my closet; I don't ever look at them, sometimes I think I ought to throw them away. But I never do.

They were what got me through elementary school, I think, and middle school for sure. What do you do when you're too smart for the freaks, but too much of a freak for the smart kids? when there's no table in the lunchroom for the ones like you?

Do you fight? or run away? or deform yourself, trying to fit in? Or do you write it all down and make stories out of it, make something out of nothing, out of sitting alone at the back of the yard wondering why no one but you can see the things you see, why no one but you gets upset when it's really cold outside, like ten below, and the animals—the birds and squirrels, the stray cats and dogs—are freezing and hungry, why no one but you is like you? Like being the last of a species, ready to go extinct; I wrote that once in one of my notebooks: *I am on the edge of extinction.* Then my stupid gym teacher saw it and called my parents: *I think Rachel has a problem with her self-esteem.* Like I was about to get all mental and go jump off the gym roof. So we had to have this stupid "intervention" meeting with the school counselor, Mr. Hile (the kids called him Hile Hitler), who told my parents— which means my mother, since Brad the Dad was as usual some-place else, on one of his many endless business trips, why does he even bother to come home?—anyway, Mr. Hile told my mother that I wasn't really self-destructive, I just needed more peer interaction. Gee, thanks, Dr. Freud. Maybe I'll go call Cara Milk-Spitter. . . . So nothing really changed, except I stopped tak-ing my notebook to gym and some kids called me crazy for a while. Big deal.

But I was talking about the shelter.

The way I found it was mostly by accident. Last year there was this Bio 1 field trip to the zoo, you would think teenagers were too old for that kind of thing, but they had us there doing "fieldwork," interviewing some of the animal-care workers; ac-tually it was pretty cool. Anyway, the guy leading the group I was in was also a shelter volunteer on weekends, and he was telling about how hard it was but how rewarding, and how he got to help place animals in new homes, and stuff like that. He had some handouts from the shelter ("Help a Pet/Save a Life"), so the next Saturday I went there, just to see.

Have you ever found something and knew it was for you? just knew it, the way a key fits in a lock? Nothing there was strange to me; it was like I'd been born there, even though at first Melissa—she's the supervisor—wasn't too sure about me, maybe because I'm young or something. But I didn't care, I just kept showing up and showing up and showing up until finally she said Oh, all right and gave me one of the green pocket aprons, and wrote me on the schedule for good.

See? I said. *I told you I belonged here.*

Well, the dogs like you, Melissa said.

It's not a fun place—no place where animals are euthanized (I won't say "put to sleep": they're not sleeping, they're *dead*) can ever be "fun"—but it's good. Cleaning them up, helping the vets, doing the feedings; I especially love doing feedings. Dogs are so happy when you feed them, it's like every good thing they can imagine rolled into one. Especially these dogs, who're used to being taken care of, belonging to someone . . . like some family who moved, or had a new baby, or just got tired of having a pet—as if a dog is a toy or an appliance or something, something you can just throw out when you don't want it anymore, just let them run loose or drop them off like garbage on our doorstep. . . . I don't know, I honestly do not know how people can be so cruel. Melissa says they have no empathy. I say they're brain-dead. These dogs are people dogs, they can't survive on their own: a car gets them, or they get sick, or starve.

But the other dogs, the born strays, the street dogs—they're different. You can't pet them, or even touch them, really. They never got used to needing people, or trusting them; they're wild.

Like the one I see when I get in today. A female collie mix, so beautiful, all gold and white and dirty; she's in the last cage on the aisle, curled up quiet, watching everything—but when I get too close she goes completely crazy, biting at the bars, herself, anything in reach, until I back off and away. Her growl's like ripping metal, jagged, dangerous, and strong; she keeps growling even as she lurches back down, half falling on an injured hind leg; I see the dressing, fresh and white, against the bars.

"Isn't she something? Like sticking your hand in a buzz saw. Lassie with an attitude." That's Jake, a big grandpa-looking guy with a thick white beard; he's about the only one, besides Melissa, that I can talk to here. When I first came I thought Oh, one big happy, because we all love animals or we wouldn't be here, right? But it was more like a hierarchy, you know, because this one's been here for five years so she gets first choice of schedule, and this one always works the Fun Run so she's in charge of that, and Don't use my clippers and I think you've got my apron and what does all this have to do with the animals anyway? So I had some trouble fitting in, as usual. Melissa says I'm "prickly." Jake says don't worry about it. I like Jake.

Now "I was out with the van last night," he tells me, leaning against one of the puppy cages, letting the puppies nip and wrestle with his fingers, strong brown fingers, gentle hands. "Out on the east side, bad neighborhood, lots of empty houses—drug houses, you know? And some kids told me about her," nodding toward the collie mix. "Hiding in this shed kind of thing, she could hardly walk on that leg—it's infected, you wouldn't believe, she must've been in a lot of pain, but man! She's a fighter all right. I had a hell of a time getting her into the van, I thought she was going to take my head off."

I lean forward, careful, ever so slightly closer; that ripping growl rises, sinks when I move back. "She's almost out of the tranks," Jake says. "Be careful, Rachel—she's wild."

Gold and white and dirty, and brown eyes, the darkest brown you ever saw, looking at me as I look at her and "That's OK," I say, to him; to her. "I'm kind of wild myself."

Language Arts, I'm sitting feet in the aisle, my prized black Converse hightops with the silver laces; Vonda Washington has to step over them to get by so "Mind moving your clown shoes?" she says; clown shoes, right. Just because they're not the sneaker of the moment. I don't get fashion, I mean I really don't. Like for a while it was wearing two T-shirts at once, a red and a black or a blue and a yellow, only certain colors with certain colors, who figures all this stuff out? who decides? Or now it's tortoiseshell everything, sunglasses, hair clips, bracelets, you name it, they wear it. I bet half of them don't even know what a tortoise is.

Now Mrs. Cruzelle's handing back papers; I get a 94 on "A Dog's Life" and a little note, *See me* in her funny handwriting so after class "Here," she says, and hands me some kind of, what is it? an entry form? "Take a look at this."

HIGH SCHOOL ESSAY CONTEST, 3,000 words max, first prize is "Susan Jardine," says Mrs. Cruzelle. "*Private Powers*, have you read it?"

That's what I like about Mrs. Cruzelle: she treats you like you have a brain, like you maybe read adult fiction for fun. "I've heard of it," I say, though I'm not sure I actually have. "It's supposed to be good."

"Oh, Jardine's an incredible writer. And she's not only judging the contest, the winner gets a private session with her, a master class up at State. . . . I really think you should enter, Rachel. With that"—pointing to "A Dog's Life" sticking out of my folder. "It needs more length, of course, and some tweaking, but I think it's a very powerful piece of work."

I look back at the entry form—*two-week intensive master class*—and "Think about it," Mrs. Cruzelle says as the bell goes off; late for Bio 2, ah crap. "And let me know what you decide."

On the way home from school I stop in at the library, looking for *Private Powers* but "It's checked out," says the guy behind the desk. His head is shaved, a smooth and gleaming cocoa-brown; he's got a tiny gold stud in his ear; his nametag says JuWan. "I can put you on the waiting list. . . . You like Susan Jardine?"

"OK, yeah. I mean, yeah, I do." All of a sudden I don't know where to look; he's smiling at me, I turn to go but "I need your card," he says, then when I don't answer, when I stand there like a moron, "Library card," he says kindly.

Of course it takes me forever to find, everything's so jumbled in my backpack—notebooks and CDs, old History papers, a bunch of shelter spay-and-neuter handouts, a mashed-up PowerBar I should really throw away—and by the time I finally dig the card out my face is bright red, I can feel it; I *hate* that. Like a big sign to the world, *Hey, look! I'm EMBARRASSED!*

"You'll get a call when the book comes in," JuWan says; he's still smiling. "Have a nice day."

Outside the air feels good, damp and chilly, cooling me down. It would have been nice to be able to talk to that guy, not to flirt or anything, but just to say something intelligent, maybe have a conversation. So why can't I talk to intelligent guys when I find them, which I almost never do? Most of the guys at my school are either jockboys or freaks or Mr. Average types who if I told them what I was thinking would just stare at me like I was from the moon, so it's not like I get a whole lot of practice. But when I do meet someone, I act like a moron. And then my mother wonders why I don't want to date.

She's home when I get there, her sky-blue van in the drive, a bunch of CAC stuff heaped on the dining room table. That's where she works, the Creative Arts Center; she helps artists get grants or something. Once or twice I went in there with her and all the people were like, *Oh, is this your daughter, the writer? Oh, you two must have so much in common!* Like what? we're both from the same end of the gene pool? They all think she's a "free spirit" because she wears chunky handmade jewelry and says "shit" out loud in the office. . . . She's not that bad, I guess, not really, but she drives me so crazy. Like the way she asks a million questions when one would do—*How are you? Are you sure? Is there anything I can do?* And she's so incredibly nervous, always wringing her hands and apologizing for one thing or another. Why does she think everything's her fault?

Like now, I can hear her on the phone: "—late last night, I'm so sorry, I should have called. But I'll be sure and stop by today, can I still pick them up today? Oh, that's great, you're such a life-saver—"

I pull out the entry form again, then "A Dog's Life"; it *needs* more *length*, so maybe I should write some about the shelter? I'll be there tomorrow, from noon till closing . . . Wonder what's up with that collie mix? Such a wild dog, the kind of dog I always wanted, *Lassie with an attitude*, which makes me laugh and "Look who's in a good mood," my mother says. With that nervous smile, like I'm a wild dog too, ready to bite if she gets an inch too close. "You must have had a good day at school."

"At my school? Not likely."

She seems like she's going to say something, then something else, then nothing; I hear her sigh. "I was going to order from Kam-Ling's for dinner, how does that sound?"

"Sounds like food." The entry form is in my hand, I could show it to her but I don't. I wonder what Susan Jardine is like? *Private Powers*, writing is a kind of private power, isn't it? And *Why, Rachel*, she says in my head, an imaginary Susan Jardine who looks vaguely like Mrs. Cruzelle, only sleeker and better dressed, *that's a wonderful insight. Your essay was also very insightful, I knew as soon as I read it that it would be the best one.*

Why, thank you. You see, I've been writing ever since I was a little kid, and—

"—cashew chicken?" My mother, loud, almost in my ear. "Rachel, cashew chicken, or what?"

"Don't scream it at me! Chicken's fine, whatever, I don't care." She finishes ordering, I hear that sigh again. "Why are we eating now?" I say, sliding the entry form back into my notebook. "It's only five-thirty, what about the missing link?"

"What?"

"Brad the Dad, remember him? Or doesn't he come home at all anymore?"

"Oh, Rachel." Now her voice is high, wavery, that underwater drowning voice. "Why do you always have to say things like that?"

"Like what? It's not my fault he's never home."

"It's no one's *fault*, it's just his job, he has to be there when they need him"—which I've heard a million times before, which I don't believe: he's a virtual guy, a computer guy, not a brain surgeon or a fireman or something; he could work from home with the computer they gave him that just sits there on his desk, or he could use his laptop. . . . He'd really rather be there than here, I wish she'd admit it for once and anyway "I don't care where he is," I say, and grabbing up my backpack and my notebook, I head past her down the hall to my room.

2

"So what's up with that collie?"

Melissa's at her desk, an old-fashioned schoolteacher's desk, dented metal drawers and heaping piles of junk: fundraising appeals, cruelty investigation forms, food orders, a busted leash tagged DON'T BUY THIS KIND!!! At the center of the heap is the brand-new computer, the one new thing in the place, a donation from some distributor. Now Melissa scrabbles like Shiva through the mess, hunting for "The pen," she says to herself, "where is the *pen?*" and then to me, "What collie?" She gives me the major Melissa stare, her wide blue eyes like *What! do! you! want!* Her hair's really, really short and blond, she gels it so it sticks up like porcupine quills. "You mean the one Jake brought in?"

"Yeah. Grrl." It was what I called her, writing last night in my paper; it fit, it's just right but "The feral one, you *named* her?" and she rolls her eyes. "Rachel, before you start, stop, all right? She's been all her life on the streets, you know what they're like when they're—"

"I know, I know." You can almost never socialize the feral ones, they're almost always euthanized. . . . I've seen dozens of dogs, and fallen in love with half of them, and cried my heart out when they died; that's how it is here. But this one is different, somehow. There's something about her, something in her eyes, I can't stop thinking about her. And I have a plan for her, or at least a plan for a plan, so "I just want to try," I say to Melissa, "just get to know her a little. And it won't interfere with my work schedule, I'll still do all my regular stuff—"

"I don't have time—*there you are!*—to argue with you now," she says, snatching up her pen. "Go away. Go talk to the dogs," which I do, sweep and swab and water and feed, all the while sneaking little looks at Grrl in her cage lying on a blue blanket, one of the old torn-up blankets from the rescue van. Her eyes are half closed, cloudy; the cage card says she's got a fever from the leg infection. When I reach to put the card back she growls at me, that ripping, ugly sound: *Don't mess with me*, that growl says. *I may be in a cage but I can still bite.*

So I start talking like I always do, to all the dogs—*Hey you guys, how's it going*—but once in a while I say "Grrl," looking into her eyes, making sure she knows it's meant for her. "Grrl, Grrl," almost like her growl but warm and crooning, the name and the idea came to me like a gift last night as I sat looking over the essay, two gifts at once because *I'm going to write about that dog*, I thought, *about Grrl*, and from "A Dog's Life" I changed the title to "straydog," all one word, the way a dog would think of herself.

And once I'd done that the words just, just *flew*, it was like I couldn't write fast enough. It was like I *knew* her, knew how she would think and feel and fear, knew it all from the inside out, and when I finally stopped writing—not done, only just started, but my hand was hot and aching and my eyes were as dry as little rubber balls—I felt so good, so . . . full, I don't know how else to explain it; like I'd eaten at a banquet, like I *was* a banquet. —Oh, that's not it either, how can words say exactly what you want sometimes and sometimes nothing at all?

Maybe I'll ask Susan Jardine.

> a hollow underpass, cars flashing, splashing by, red-lights, whitelights, bright. no one notices me, brown eyes and wet paws, long fur going every which way: straydog, They say that. is that me?
>
> stray, runaway. i run and run till my pads, paws, are sore, leather cracked and nails dull against the hard ground, hard like stone in long lines, softer on grass, weeds, leaves i sniff and dig through: find a sandwich squashed in a paper sack, meat bread yellow smear, two bites and gone.
>
> still hungry. hungry is a place inside, empty as a world. can it be filled up? i don't know.
>
> home is noplace, a place where i once was, was that a home? box full of rags, soft and damp, smell like soap and They and us, all of us: little ones like me, nip teeth and push, wriggle, wiggle; and a big one, milk, warm and safe. good smells.
>
> then: oh then *gone*, food warm good all gone, the big one too, the box, the other little ones and me out

19

cold and wandering, pads sore, and crying, crying for the big one, for what was not anymore. leaves, i remember leaves wet and chill against my fur, dark beneath the trees and something biting my back, biting hard, and me biting back at it just as hard, AFRAID, taste in my mouth like old bad meat and then the thing was gone; i was gone; all gone.

where from then? just out, still out: into cold and dark, noplace to stay, keep moving moving moving. hard stone ground, square box of buildings, sometimes empty, sometimes filled with They so I moved on, looking and looking, not finding; alone.

where tonight? i don't know. i just know now, the street, wet, flea crawl and flicking ears. a place to sleep, maybe, by the big square metal thing They dump food in; behind it is sometimes safe. sometimes.

once, in the box, i was safe. the big warm one made me warm, i slept with my ears down, slept whenever i wanted to. not now. now sleep is when i have to, and always ears-up, listening: for danger, rocks ropes cars mean ones like me; They.

some like me live with They, walk with They, tied to They. They have food and give it, i know, maybe all you want—but to stay by They, when They can—They do—hit, hurt, drag, throw things, scare and scare? *no*. i won't eat from They hands, i won't be tied to They when They can hurt so fast, before you even know what's happening.

so in this wet dark i sit, watching. a cat goes by, quick feet small, low to the ground; i hear the cat pass. i don't hunt cats, some like me do but i don't. other noises, metal noises, loud; one of They comes to the metal square, throws white bags smashed crushed plastic not-good-to-eat, but with some food inside; i know. when that They is gone i can check, and see, and eat.

until then i wait, wet, ears up. something else, rat? small, heads for the metal square, and i growl to make it move, go the other way. there is no share, no you-have-i-have. not enough food, ever, so there has to be growling and biting, even for the small ones, cat rat even smaller, all of them, even the ones like me. only They will always have enough.

hill morning storm, a spring storm half snow and half rain, my hightops are soaked. I should have let my mother drive me, but the way she said it—*Don't you want a ride?* like I might expire or something if I walked—got my back up, so I said no. And now my hair is plastered to my head and I'm freezing. Maybe there's such a thing as being too independent.

In the halls are Day-Glo posters—RETRO DANCE, DON'T FORGET!!—and in the morning announcements some girl urges everyone to "make sure and get your tickets today!" Across the aisle Chelsea and Courtney murmur about who's asking who and what they'll wear and blah blah blah and so on. Mrs. Cruzelle has to be stern to get everyone focused, and then just as she begins to talk about the new section we're starting (it's called "Shakespeare's Women," like Juliet, ugh, but Portia and Lady Macbeth, yay juicy), the door opens and in comes this guy.

Tall, taller than me, raveled black sweatshirt, a mop of very blond hair, but he walks like a ghost, just drifting in as if it doesn't matter if he's in the room, any room, or not; his backpack looks realer than he does, big and knobby, hung on his shoulders like a turtle's shell. He mumbles something to Mrs. Cruzelle, hands her a pink late slip, then drifts to a seat on the other side of the room, the window side, where he stares into the parking lot. Another Lost Boy.

It's a name I made up, a category; we're all in categories here whether we want to be or not, so I made up some of my own. The TV Girls, like Chelsea and Courtney and Vonda Washington, are like the girls on the teen sitcoms: perfect looks, hair, clothes, even perfect problems, like Which guy should I jerk around this week? Their boyfriends are of course the TV Guys, same deal except their problems are more like Should I be captain of the basketball or football team? Or both?

Then there's the honor-roll group, or the People from the Planet Mensa; they're in Honors everything, and they all want to be valedictorian and go to Harvard. I don't mind them too much, but in their own way they're as cliquish as the TV people, and maybe even more competitive. Although at least they never ask me for test answers.

The biggest group are the Walla-Wallas, the regular people. I call them that because I once read that in movies the people in crowd scenes, at restaurants or parties, are told to say "wallawalla" instead of real conversation so it just sounds like a murmur, without any actual words. Which is kind of what you hear in the halls: walla-walla, nothing distinct, everybody looking and dressing and thinking like everybody else. These guys are only dangerous in a stampede.

After them come the Creatives, the ones who spend their lunch hour in the art room; and the Net Jockeys, the computer room, laptop heaven. Then come the losers, the junior alcoholics and the proto-junkies; I call them the Code Blues.

Last of all are the Lost Boys (and Girls): the ones on the margins, the ones who never answer back, who float like flotsam down the halls. They get on my nerves, for some reason; maybe because they're so completely passive. I mean, get up on your hind legs sometimes, OK? Fight back a little, take a stand, make yourself heard.

Which is why I now and always will ignore this new kid, Lost Boy in his window seat, ignoring everything back—the world, the class, Mrs. Cruzelle, who I'm dying to talk to about my essay-in-progress—until class is over and I head for her desk but somehow he gets there before me, shuffling up with some papers in his hand, all creased and crappy from his backpack and "Let me see those, Griffin," says Mrs. Cruzelle, so I can either hang around like a barnacle and be late, again, for Bio 2, or move on, which is what I end up doing after giving an evil look to Mr. Lost Boy for getting in my way.

And the next day is even worse, because—in early, hurrying from my locker to catch her before class—just as I'm pulling out my essay Mrs. Cruzelle asks, "Can I partner you with Griffin?" She means editing partner, since Courtney, Chelsea, and Jon just have to be a threesome, making me the odd one out in the room—no surprise, and it doesn't bother me, Mrs. Cruzelle edits my stuff herself. But now "He's a top-notch writer," she says, "but he needs to get up to speed in the class. Would you mind, Rachel?"

Yes, I would, actually, even though I don't say that to her, I don't say anything beyond a sketchy shrug. And then she asks, "Have you thought about that essay contest at all?" so finally I can show her what I've got, it's all rough draft but "Oh, terrific," she says, smiling down at the pages as if they're some rare treasure—and she means it too, I know she does because she always says that good writing makes her happy, whether it's by Shakespeare, or me, or whoever; she says it's why she became a teacher in the first place. Makes you wonder why she didn't become a writer instead.

So I don't feel quite as snarky about Lost Boy, I mean Griffin. And when it's time to do editing I go over to where he's sitting, half turned toward the window, and say "Listen," reaching for his two and a half grubby pages. "This is how it works: I read your stuff, and you read my stuff, and then we critique. OK?" Eyes half shut, he takes "straydog"; we're supposed to be doing a personal essay, but I didn't have time to write anything else and anyway it's very personal already.

Feet crossed, purple felt-tip in hand, I start reading his stuff, ready to correct, suggest, whatever . . . but after about two minutes "I can't do anything with this," I say, showing him the unmarked pages; I have to say it twice, to get him to look at me. "There's nothing here."

He doesn't answer, only gives me The Stare, blank and half-mast. "Mrs. Cruzelle says you're really good," I say, handing back his pages. "But this is like—'Personally I have no personal opinions,' what kind of crap is that? Give me something I can work with, OK?"

He still doesn't say anything, just turns back to "straydog," scratch-scratch-scratch until the bell goes, then he hands me my pages and goes off without a word.

I forget about it till lunch, rain and snow over for now so I head for the steps, sun and clouds in drifting bands, the parking-lot trees like stark charcoal lines drawn on a pale gray watercolor sky. After my orange muffin and Cappuccino Swirl— I believe I may be addicted to Cappuccino Swirls—I finally take out "straydog," ready to erase whatever Griffin wrote. But before I do, I read: *need more descrip.* in messy cursive, *what kind dog?* in the margin, *how's it end?* at the end and "Hey," someone says, *he says,* Griffin Lost Boy standing over me, squinting in the sun that makes him a silhouette, dark, a shape without features. "Check this," and he hands me some pages, new pages, he must have just printed them out—and then is gone, shuffling up the stairs, back into the building like a prisoner heading back to his cell.

I don't bother with the pages until late that night, after dinner (my mother rushing in with takeout chicken—*Oh, I'm sorry, the traffic on Bretnor was just horrible, let me just stick this in the microwave*— while Brad stares at the TV), after homework (an evolution paper for Bio 2, a three-page printout for Psych, blah, and a pretest in History, did I remember my history book? no, I did not), after falling half asleep brushing my teeth . . . But how long can it take to plow through more nothing? So I pull the pages out of where I crammed them in my backpack, uncrease them, and start reading—

—and forget, after a minute, that I'm reading at all, just let myself be carried by the voice on the page: a dark, sure voice talking pure space-poetry, all about black holes and dark matter and wormholes into your mind, like consciousness is space, how does he put it? "Every brain a universe." And the way he writes—it's almost like spoken-word stuff, or haiku, spare and brief but, but beautiful too, in the way lightning is beautiful, or the white curve of a skull, or the idea of neutrinos, tiny tiny things always passing through everything else, coming from where nobody knows. . . . And all of this came out of Griffin Lost Boy? Unbelievable. No wonder Mrs. Cruzelle said he was a good writer. He's as good as me.

Which might sound snobby, maybe, but it's really not. When you can do something pretty well, the knowledge of how hard it is to do it, and how much work it really takes to get it right, makes you a better judge of someone else's ability, makes you appreciate when something is really good. Like I can appreciate this stuff.

So when I mark it up, my comments are mostly compliments, except for the spelling; he's a truly atrocious speller. And the next day in class I go right over to him and "Hey," I say. "These"—holding out the pages, shaking them a little so they rattle like dry leaves—"are *amazing*. And weird."

"Amazingly weird," he says, looking past me out the window; his eyes, up close, are a wary gray. "That's me."

"No, I mean it, how did you learn to write like that? How did you—" but Mrs. Cruzelle is trying hard for quiet, "Class, *class*," so I cross the room, Griffin's pages still in hand, plop in my seat to hear "Clath, clath, thit down," from Jon Truman to Chelsea, who gives her obnoxious bimbo giggle. "Thit in your *theatth*." They see me looking—glaring—at them and "Thut up," Chelsea says to me, loud, and they both laugh, how can they not care if she hears? How can they not care about anyone but themselves?

27

If Mrs. Cruzelle does hear them she doesn't react, just starts people reading from their papers, first page only and "Put a little feeling into it," she says, in a pleading kind of way; she looks tired today. "This is about you, remember?"

So I think about Grrl as I read my page, tough lost beautiful Grrl, hiding, hurt, defiant in a drug-house shed, fighting the people who only want to help. When I finish Mrs. Cruzelle says, "Terrific!" which makes me smile, a couple of kids nod until Courtney says, "So Rachel, you're, what, a dog?" and everybody laughs, well not everybody, Mrs. Cruzelle doesn't laugh and neither does Griffin—who, when it's his turn, reads his stuff in the blankest, dullest voice imaginable, as if it were stock market numbers or the phone book. I could punch him for ruining it that way.

Then when he finishes, slumping back in his seat "What's that supposed to mean?" Jon Truman says in a complaining tone, like he bought a new shirt and it didn't fit. "First someone's a dog, and then this one's a space alien or something, I thought we were supposed to be writing about ourselves—"

"Then you should've turned in a blank sheet of paper," I say, harsh as Grrl's ripping growl; someone behind me gives a smothered little laugh but it's not a joke, I'm too mad for jokes, *mad dog* and "Just because you can't understand something," I say, my voice getting louder, "doesn't give you the right to trash it. Just because you're too st—"

"Stop it, Rachel," says Mrs. Cruzelle; her face is calm but her voice is hard. "We critique work here, not personalities. Jon, see me after class."

"Me? She's the one who—"

"See me after class," and now her face is hard too, staring at him until he backs down. When she looks away he flips me off, but I don't care; screw you back, Jon Truman, you TV Boy wannabe, you couldn't write like Griffin if you lived a million years.

At lunch it's raining again, a drifting mist, so I head instead for the Media Center and hole up in one of the carrels, where I try to write in my notebook, but I'm still too mad so I end up doodling, ugly little pictures until "Hey," from behind me; it's Griffin. "Thought you'd be dukin' it out in the cafetorium with Joe Primetime. . . . Want some?" holding out a bag of chips. Suddenly I'm hungry so we sit there eating, you're not supposed to eat in the Media Center but no one's paying any attention and we finish the bag, not talking, just watching the rain until "This school," he says, as if he's talking to himself, "is just like my last one. I thought when I got out of Burgess—"

"You went to Burgess? Wow. That's a gifted school, it's—"

"Gifted, sure . . . You want some of these GummiWorms?" Rain on the windows, river on river on river, coursing down. "It's still bullshit. They tell you they want you to think for yourself, but when you do, bam."

"Mrs. Cruzelle," I say, "is OK. But the rest of them mostly suck."

"Yeah. Just like at Burgess. Or like with my horn. —Trumpet," his fingers wiggling in empty air, as if he's playing. "The music guy here wants me to join the marching band, but I told him there's no way I'm going to wear some stupid uniform and hop around a football field just so I can play my horn. . . . So I guess I'm not playing."

29

"So what are you doing?"

"Nothing," he says, and makes a smile, not a happy smile. "Just doin' my jail time."

GummiWorm stuck on my teeth, too sweet, like chewing glue; I used to dream of going to Burgess, I thought it would be like getting out of jail. . . . "Your dog thing was really good," Griffin says. "Was that, is that your dog?"

Grrl, in her cage. Last night I dreamed I took her home; only a dream, right? Or could I really do it? If I put in tons of face time with her, got her used to me, got her trusting me. . . . I couldn't bring her in the house, my mother's head would probably explode or something—but what about in the back yard? Once I got her trusting me, got her to stop being afraid—

But Griffin's still looking at me, head to one side so "No," I say through half-stuck Gummi teeth; should I tell him about Grrl? "Well, yes and no—" as the bell goes off, I bend for my notebook and "See you later," he says, and is gone, through the door and merging with the moving Walla-Wallas, blond head and black sweatshirt disappearing down the hall.

a They in a car is looking at me.

cars are bad. too big, smell bad, run too fast, run you over without even trying; and no bite will hurt a car.

the car moves, moves at me and i *run*, claws pads scrabble, hard ground dirt weeds the broken shine that cuts, cuts up your paws if you step on it, like ice but it never melts. i run till i know the car is gone,

30

then stand panting in an alley, ribs in and out in and out, hot breath, hot all over. i need water.

so i go looking sniffing, throat so dry, worse almost than hungry to be thirsty; almost. once in bad thirst i drank green water, two licks bright green and sweet and it made me sick, sick like claws digging in my belly, so sick i almost closed my eyes always. more careful now, i search, sniff, dry tongue in dry mouth till finally by a food place i find water, brown trickled pond by one of the metal squares, i drink it all . . . then find behind the square, oh! a whole chicken! so *good* and i eat quick quick to make sure no one takes it, eat it all and some of its paper skin too.

hungry is a place to get out of, so big i think i never can get out. the only thing bigger than hungry is AFRAID. AFRAID is bigger than anything, black like night that never stops, dark in the head and in the dark can be anything: They, car, green water, anything. only running keeps AFRAID away.

now a tiny flea-crawl up my back, i scratch good and hard, sniff to make sure there's no more food; no, all gone so i go too, claw click as a They comes out of the food place, shouts at me—*hey, git! straydog*—but much too far to catch or grab, i growl as i go but mostly i trot because it feels good, my belly full, sun warm on my fur, not a bad day to be straydog.

4

It's only seven Saturday morning but I'm up already, I want to get to the shelter early today. I crave some coffee but the grinder's too loud, so I make instant instead, bleah. The light in the kitchen is a pale yellow, a peaceful color, like the quiet of the house around me. During the week, mornings are a nightmare, me and my mother fighting for the bathroom—it takes her forever to put on her makeup—but now it's all calm and still.

Outside is cloudy, lots of little clouds in lines: a mackerel sky, they call that. The window thermometer says forty-eight degrees; chilly on my bike. I can't wait to do driver's training next year, get a car, get mobile. . . . Jelly toast for now, PowerBar for later, I eat standing up looking out at the back yard. The honeysuckle vines are dark, leaves drooping from winter's touch; the three bird feeders need to be filled again. My mother buys the big thirty-pound bags of seed, but the birds go through it fast when it's cold.

Now I hear her coming down the stairs; she's dressed already, flowing skirt and one of those overly fuzzy sweaters that make her look like she's being mugged by a pastel bear. She's putting on earrings when she looks up and sees me, and stops.

"Well, good morning. You're up early."

"Shelter day," I say, and stuff down the rest of my toast. She fills the red teapot—she's not a coffee fiend like me—and slices an orange; the scent fills the kitchen, and all of a sudden I remember how she used to cut up fruit for me, oranges, apples, to make them look like little flowers, fruit-flowers on a blue kiddie plate; wonder what happened to that plate? My gaze on her is sideways, she doesn't see me so I can really look at her, observe her as if I've never seen her before: the tired lines in her face, the gray hair starting; she doesn't dye her hair, and I'm glad. The gray is soft and silvery, like frost on a window when the sun hits, like a decoration, so much nicer than, say, those dumb chandelier earrings she likes. I wonder how I'll look when I'm her age, a million years from now. Will my hair be gray too? Will I have those same lines in my forehead, that same small defeated frown? I read once that when you grow up you get the face you deserve, but does she deserve to look so sad? . . . But now she's looking at me, so I look away.

"Do you need a ride?" she asks, reaching for a cup: pale blue china, the same color as her eyes. "I'm leaving in a few minutes."

"I'll ride my bike."

"All right," with a sigh; the water's just about boiling. "Have a good day," she says, and "You too," I say back, which seems to startle her: and then she smiles, a smile I don't see too often.

"Thanks," she says. "I'll try."

As I drag my bike out of the garage, I have to maneuver around Brad's new toy, a flashy metallic-green Jeep with oversize tires, it looks like one of those stupid monster-truck things shrunk to regular size. Plus it cost, like, a mint, I heard them arguing about it, my mother all anxious, *Do we really want to spend so much on a car?* and Brad saying, *I work hard, Elisha, I need to reward myself.* He always makes it seem like whatever he's saying is the way things really are, and if you disagree, you're stupid or crazy or irrational. This bothers her a lot, I know—she's always trying to justify herself to him—but it doesn't bother me. I don't agree with him on *anything*, and I couldn't care less what he thinks.

Down the driveway and into the street, my backpack thumps gently on my shoulders as I ride; I've got treats inside, Wagalong treats for Grrl. Food is love to animals. So if I keep feeding her, and talking to her, and getting a little closer each time . . . there'll be *some* response, anyway, right? There has to be.

The shelter smells like dog, and cat, and cleaning stuff; it's still pretty quiet, with only the occasional bark, or the tiny, bewildered mewing of the kittens—we got a litter of kittens the other day; this woman and her kids brought them in. The kids were crying, but the woman was all annoyed: *I can't imagine how Bootsy got pregnant* . . . Oh, probably the usual way, lady. She was in heat and you let her out because you couldn't handle watching her pace and cry, and boom, here's six kittens nobody wants. Spay or neuter, spay or neuter, no matter how many times you tell them they don't listen. They should have to come in and watch when we euthanize, maybe that would get it through

34

their heads. Have you ever seen a dead kitten? How about six dead kittens? If your heart doesn't break then, you don't have one. No wonder the shelter staff get schizo sometimes—you would be too if you had to live every day on that balance, loving the animals but having to kill them. Even if it's the only alternative to a short and cruel life on the streets, it feels horrible anyway. And the whole thing's just because of ignorance, people's ignorance . . . They need to be educated. They need to be hit on the head with a board. Like Melissa keeps saying, "Knowledge saves lives."

Right now no one's in yet but her: I can hear her banging around in her office, yelling at the computer, "What is *wrong* with this thing!" so I shrug off my backpack and step in to help.

As usual she's trying to do too many things at once, and crashing, so I back her up and start over again. That's Melissa, though, she always does too many things at once, mostly because she has to: be the boss, and the mommy, and the cop, talk to Animal Control, set up satellite adoptions, handle the money from the Fun Run, screen new volunteers . . . *and* keep the old ones happy, *and* order supplies, *and* write fundraising letters—which is what she was trying to do when she crashed. "Sit Up and Beg!" it says at the top, with a graphic of a tail-wagging dog, and "You're not on the schedule till noon," she says, reaching gloomily for her coffee, a chipped white cup that reads BROOK-DALE ANIMAL SHELTER. "Did you come to check up on your protégée?"

I don't say anything. *Sit up, roll over, play dead, we'll do whatever it takes to get your donation!*

"You know it's not going to work, Rachel. You have to be realistic, for your own sake. And for the dog's. She's miserable here, or haven't you noticed?"

"Your file's OK now," I say. My voice is flat; I try not to sound the way I feel. I mean, I'm not stupid, I realize that Grrl's got problems, big problems, but it's not like it never ever happens, a street dog adopted out. In fact I saw it happen myself, not with a dog but with these cats that we rescued from a "collector," you know about collectors? It's a real mental disorder, a collector just keeps taking in more and more strays, but doesn't care for them—or can't—so the animals live in terrible conditions. Like with these cats: the neighbors called the cops because they thought somebody had died in the house, the smell was so rank. But really it was about thirty cats, with no litterboxes, and rotten food crusted all over everything, and this old half-blind lady sitting in the middle of it and talking about her "babies." Most of them had to be euthanized, they were either so sick we couldn't help them or so undersocialized that they were totally feral. But Katie—she's been here forever, we call her Grandma Katie—she worked with three of the youngest ones—a calico, a kind of Maine Coon mix, and a tiger—like I want to do with Grrl, and in the end we were able to place them after all. So what I'm asking isn't totally impossible, just hard. Very hard, OK, I admit it. But—

"Rachel," Melissa says now, "that dog's feral, all right? Not just undersocialized, *feral*. She's not ever going to be adoptable, by you or anyone else. You're just fooling yourself."

My hands are shaking, trembling at my sides; I can feel the

anger in me, anger and something else. We've had run-ins be-fore, like over the adoption policies, or what I can and can't do with the dogs, but this is different. And she knows it's different, I can hear it in her voice, see it in her wide eyes wider than ever as "I'm doing this on my own time," I say, loud. "So what dif-ference does it make if—"

"It makes a difference to the dog. And it's tight here, we need to give the space to animals we can place, not the ones who—"

"I'll bring in a cage, then!" Now I'm so mad I feel tears in my eyes, hot-metal tears like solder and my face is hot too, hot and white like a skull in the desert, I hear my own voice loud and hollow, a skull's voice. "We're supposed to be saving animals, not killing them!"

"I would save them all if I could!" Her voice is louder now too, almost as loud as mine. "But I can't. And neither can you. It's triage, we have to do what's possible—"

But I can't listen anymore, if I do I'll scream or cry, I have to get out of here—but as I storm out of the office I run right into Jake, travel mug in hand, coffee steam and "Whoa!" he says, grabbing my arm to steady me, himself. "Sorry, sorry—" Then he sees my face, my eyes, looks quickly past me to Melissa and "Scuse us," he says to her, and shuts the door. Then, still holding my arm: "What happened?"

I will not cry; I will not cry—but I can't talk either, I can barely breathe so "Come here," he says and tows me gently to the exam room, metal-topped table, shelves full of swabs and sharps and tubes of NutriCal. "Now tell me. What happened?"

So I tell him, in short, hard bursts, it's hard even to start talking but once I do I can; the pressure in my chest, behind my eyes, eases a little. And he listens, arms crossed, leaning against the table, just listens and doesn't say anything until he's sure that I'm done. Then "My sister," he says, "used to crate her Newfie, Edgar. Biggest dog you ever saw. She might still have the cage."

He picks up his travel mug, heads out of the room; I hear him cross the hall to Melissa's office, then their voices, hers sharp, his low, but I don't want to hear any more so I go do what I came to do, which is see Grrl: curled in the cage, dirty gold-and-white and just the sight of her calms me, those dark, fierce, knowing eyes. Her leg dressing is soiled but the leg itself looks better, no more swelling as far as I can see. Slowly, very slowly, I sit down, not next to the cage but on the floor before it, just sit there and listen to her growl. I know just how she feels—trapped; helpless; filled with an anger as big as she is so she's like a glass overflowing. . . . See the look in her eyes, as if she were far, far back in a cave, the cave of herself, the only safe place in the world; it breaks my heart to see it. She doesn't know that I want more than anything to help her, to be a safe place. To her I'm just another bad thing, an enemy, a They.

So I start talking again, quiet and slow, just about nothing, just her name, over and over again: like a song, a little song from me to her, as I reach into my backpack and dig out the Wagalongs. I know she can smell them, I can see it in her eyes, but when I put out my hand the growls are snarls are bared teeth and lips skinned back, her whole body is rigid, ready to leap so "OK," I say, "OK, Grrl, OK," and just pour out a handful close enough for her to reach through the bars. Then I sit back, and wait; and wait; but the growling never stops, her ears never come up so "OK," I say again, backpack up and out of the room—to peek around the door and watch her wolf up the treats, long collie nose desperate to sniff and find them all.

For the rest of my shift I avoid Melissa, and glare at her when I can't. *Don't worry*, I keep telling myself, *Grrl's going to be OK*. Meanwhile I do the job, clean the runs, fill the bowls and "Hey," says Jake as he passes me with an armload of paper towels, "you know that boxer? the parking-lot one? He was adopted out yesterday, to a real nice couple, an older couple. Said he looked just like their old dog Peanuts."

The boxer was found loose in a parking lot, abandoned or a runaway: big and gorgeous, pure hyper in that young-dog way; Jake smiles and so do I. That's the best part of being here, all the happy endings: the puppy rescued from a storm drain, the three Siamese adopted out together, the old deaf Lab chosen *because* he's old and deaf: *He needs somebody*, the guy had said, rubbing the Lab's back as the dog wagged his tail, slow and calm and wondering, his future changing all around him. When these things happen my heart fills up, like when I'm writing but in a different way: it's soft, and it aches, but a beautiful ache, as if the happiness is more precious because I know things could have so easily gone the other way: the puppy drowned, the cats separated, the Lab euthanized because no one wanted an old deaf dog. It's like the pain is a splinter in the joy, a dark vein in a sea of gold, but only both of them together can teach you how sweet the joy really is.

That kind of joy is coming for Grrl too, I know; it has to. Before I leave I check on her again: she sees me peek around the door and the growl rises in her chest, still buzz saw but maybe—maybe?—not quite so loud. I picture her out in the sunshine, fur clean, chasing a Frisbee or a squirrel; or sprawled out sleeping on my bed, her paws twitching lightly as she dreams.

Don't worry, Grrl, don't worry. I'm going to take you home.

5

"More dog stuff?" says Griffin as I hand him some pages. His are titled "Those Amazing Assholes," which makes me smile. My eyes are burning, I didn't sleep too well last night, but once I start reading I forget that I'm tired, forget the class around me, just read and try not to burst out laughing. It's completely hilarious, all about these teen zombies who try to take over the world but can't because they're too busy shopping or watching TV, the whole thing written in a kind of commercial-speak, like *Whitney's beautiful, tangle-free hair swings in the wind as she eats her fill of delicious lo-cal, no-cal human flesh!*

"You like?" Griffin says into my ear. Today he's wearing fatigue pants and a Peppy's Pizza T-shirt, Peppy the Clown in garish red and green. "I thought you might."

"It's amazing! It's—"

" 'Those Amazing Assholes,' " he says in a deep announcer's voice, then goes back to my pages.

As the bell goes he gathers his stuff, then waits at the door; is he waiting for me? but Mrs. Cruzelle motions me over, she probably wants to talk about the essay contest so "See you at lunch?" I say to him, did he hear me? but he's gone.

Mrs. Cruzelle has a Susan Jardine book to give me, it's called On the Matter of My Suicide but "It's a comedy," says Mrs. Cruzelle, smiling. "A black comedy. It's very funny. . . . How's the essay coming?"

"Good." It's weird, but the more I worry about Grrl, the better the writing seems to get, as if the worry, the feelings, are an engine driving the words; and the writing makes me feel like it can happen, it will happen, I'll get her out of there and bring her home somehow. Somehow. Yesterday I looked online for dog supplies, crates, do-it-yourself kennels. Also muzzles. "I should have it done pretty soon."

"I'd like to review it before you send it, if that's OK with you. —How are things working out with Griffin?"

"Really good," I say. "He's a great writer."

At lunch I head straight for the Media Center, but Griffin's not there. I check the carrels, the computers, where could he be? Maybe he didn't hear me; maybe he heard me and didn't care. Well, fine, I can eat lunch alone, I've done it a million times. I just thought that he—

"Hey," from behind me, it's him, he's out of breath. "It's nice outside, I thought you'd be out on the steps." He's got two bags of chips today, we go by the windows to eat and "Your dog thing," he says. "That's a real dog, right? But not your dog?"

I look past him, out the window. Today there's a wind in the trees, old dead leaves torn free and sent flying: like thoughts, dreams, days in the future, things that will happen that right now we can't see. He's waiting but I don't say anything, not sure how much to tell him, how much I want to tell. He doesn't push, he eats a chip, he offers me some of his green mango tea until finally "She's at the shelter," I say, "at Brookdale, where I work. She's this beautiful collie mix, but she's a street dog, feral, you know? When they get like that they're hard to tame, really hard because they don't trust anybody, they've had it too bad, too many people have been mean to them. . . ." My voice is rising, heads are turning our way so "I want her," I say, more quietly. "But I don't know if she'll ever trust me enough."

He takes out a Hershey bar, breaks it in two and "Doesn't it bother you?" he asks, head to one side; he's got an earring under all that blond, a tiny silver skull and crossbones. The candy is soft and sweet, melting on my tongue, melting into nothing; outside a car goes by, the bass so loud you can feel it in the glass. "To work there and see that? Abused animals, and all?"

"Yeah it bothers me, I hate it. I hate the people who hurt them, too." There are stories I could tell him, but I won't, they're too terrible, too sad. But "I go there to take care of them, to—love them. And it isn't all sad either." I tell him about the boxer and the three Siamese, about the old deaf Lab and "It keeps me going," I say, "when things work out. And I know things are going to work out with—" Grrl "—the collie. I just have to keep trying." No matter what Melissa says.

The bell goes off then, startling us both; it doesn't seem like lunch should be over already. One of the media aides sees Griffin throwing away the Hershey's wrapper and gives us the two-minute lecture on This Is Not the Cafeteria, and Griffin says,

"Yeah, I know, the people in here can read," which makes me laugh, which makes the aide write both of us up. Or down.

At the stairway he's going one way, I'm going the other so "Thanks for the Hershey," I say. "See you tomorrow."

"Sure," he says, and then stops, standing there in the rush and crush of Walla-Wallas like a person stuck in a fast-moving river, mouth open as if he's going to say something else, like what? But then he doesn't, just melts into the crowd and is gone—

—until after school, by the east doors, hands in his pockets, sun on his hair the color of, what? of wheat? of dandelion fluff? and "Are you going today?" he says, falling into step with me. "To see your dog?"

I slow then stop in the midst of the sidewalk traffic; I can feel my face getting hot. I don't know what to do. In my backpack are more Wagalongs and a book I brought to read aloud to Grrl; I've heard that trainers do that sometimes, to get a dog accustomed to the trainer's voice. It's not that I'm embarrassed to do it in front of Griffin, but—but what? I don't know. It's just that the shelter is my place, my safe space, and to let someone, anyone, come in. . . . But I don't want to lie about where I'm going, either, not to Griffin. A hundred things cross my mind, like water striders on the surface of a pond, frantic and swift—*what if he laughs what if he tells tells who no one cares about you here no one cares what you do*—

—and he sees it in my face, he must have because his own face starts closing, his smile falters and "Never mind," he says, taking a step back, away from me. "See you tomorrow."

I feel like I'm on the edge of a cliff: my heart is beating like a fist in my chest, knocking, pounding and "You want to go with me to the shelter?" I say, each word like a step into nothing, into thin air. "Come on."

I start walking; will he follow? and he does, saying nothing, backpack hung from one lean shoulder, both of us in step now as we cross the parking lot, elm leaves lost to last year's cold a carpet to the street.

> now i hide, have to hide, can't run or even walk far without hurt, so much hurt in my leg! hurt and AFRAID.
>
> at first just hungry, loping in long sun-shadows, night coming soon. dirt weeds old box-buildings, They-stuff scattered all over the ground and some They sitting on a car, smoke-smell and something bad beneath, very bad, a smell like AFRAID and *hey Lassie,* says a They, rising from its place, *c'mere I got something for you.*
>
> the laughing sound, but not a happy sound: I growl, back up, ready to run—but from where i don't see comes another They, a sick one, it hardly stands on its own: stagger and stink, hand almost on my back and i *bite,* bite so it leaves me, the They cries out—
>
> —and another They hits at me, hard in the leg like a bite, bad bite so i turn to run but my leg, oh! the hurt, i fall and the They kicks at me, kicks my belly, i scramble claws against the ground and a harsh sound, short, like a breaking stick, hits close to me, dirt and pebbles fly—

45

—but now i'm up, belly sore and hard to breathe, try to run again but i can't run

AFRAID

i can't run

AFRAID OH

but i can move, limp stagger like the sick They, leg dragging, blood-smell and hurt but AFRAID gets smaller as i move, fast as i can to find a place to hide, to lick and sniff my leg, hide till i can run again.

i find a small box-building, it smells of They but gone-away They, very gone so i can hide there. belly flat, ears down, sound in my throat like the hurt in my leg; finally i sleep. waking in the dark i hear cat sounds, a caught squeaking, mouse or rat? my belly hurts where the They kicked me but no blood there, my belly is fine. my leg is bad, AFRAID bad, cut deep.

i sleep again, wake in the light and thirsty now, oh, bad thirsty, worse even than hungry, but when i try to walk i fall so i have to wait. the sun moves; the light passes. They go by, close and far, They don't see me in here. when i hear no They for a time, long time, i creep out and try to find water, even green water, something to drink because i have to drink.

i find some, not too far: in weeds, a crushed cup . . . and back to where i was, lying still, breathing in and out. very hungry now, hungry-sick but no way to hunt food; my leg is worse, fat and red at the bite; a poison bite? AFRAID waits, crouched like They, waiting for me to come out so it can hurt me again.

All the way to the shelter he asks me questions, like how I started working there, and what it's like, and what we do: we help animals, I tell him, we just do what we can. And then I tell him the starfish story, you know that story? A guy's walking on a beach where the tide's gone out, leaving thousands of starfish stranded, so as he walks he picks one up, and another, and another, and throws them back into the water. Another guy sees him doing this and says, Hey, there's a million of those things, just throwing a few of them back won't make any difference. And the first guy holds up a starfish, throws it back into the sea, and says, It made a difference to that one.

"That's what we do," I say.

When we get there it's not too busy so I can show him all around: here's where we do intake, here's the rescue vans, here's the dog side, the cat side and "All those kittens," he says; he sounds flat and airless, like someone who's just been punched. I forget how overwhelming this place can be if you're not used to it. "What hap—" and then he stops, he knows what happens to them, some of them; most of them. There's just too many, too many . . . and "Hey, hey," his face close to the cage bars, letting two kittens sniff his fingertips; his voice is very soft. "Hey, little guys."

With him here the place seems, I don't know, a little shabbier; it is pretty shabby, I guess. Whatever money comes in goes to the animals, so the walls need painting (not the same hospital-puke green, thank you very much), and the floor is grimy and scuffed—but he's not looking at any of that, he's still looking at the kittens and his face is as soft as his voice, a look I haven't seen before: like the real Griffin's come to the surface, come out

47

of hiding as he pets the kittens, murmurs to them—and then he sees me looking and blushes, an actual blush, it makes me smile: You like kittens, huh? Well, your dark secret's safe with me.

"Cats are cool," he says, as if he has to justify himself; I'm still smiling, I don't say anything but "Want to see her now?"

We cross over to the dog side; a few new ones have come in since I was here last—an old-looking poodle, a big slaphappy mutt—now every cage is full but I don't think about that, not now, I can't and "There she is," I say, proud. "That's Grrl."

He goes cautiously to the cage, not too close, not too fast but of course she's growling already, a long, strong growl, it cuts through the others' barking like a knife. "Careful," I warn him. "She's pretty wild."

"I know. I read the story, remember? . . . Hey there, lady," he says to Grrl, in the kitten-voice, the kind voice, the voice that says, I will *never ever* hurt you. Jake told me once that only people who've been hurt know what it means to be kind. I wonder if Jake's coming in today. I wonder if he got that cage from his sister, and what I'm going to do if he didn't . . . Buy one, I guess, and pretty quick, Grrl's obviously getting stronger, she can stand up again and stay up, even though she's wobbly, she's standing up now and—

"Man!" as Griffin jerks away, hard, from the bars, the way you jump back from fire, or out of the path of a car: he hadn't tried to touch her but she went for him anyway, teeth bare, her growl pure snarl—and he's looking at me with wide eyes, like I might think it was his fault: "I didn't touch her, Rachel, honest, I didn't even try to—"

"I know." She's sitting down again, snarl gone back to growl and for a moment my heart sinks, a mineshaft feel, falling and falling: *it's triage, we have to do what's possible* but she can't help the way she is, she can't help it! Are we going to kill her for being what she is, what people have made her? People, and hunger, and nights on the street, if she hadn't learned to fight she'd've disappeared a long time ago . . . but she *has* to learn to change now, she has to change or she'll die, how can I make her understand that? and "Hey," Griffin says, soft, like the kitten-voice in my ear. "It's OK. She just—surprised me."

Tears in my eyes, I don't want him to see. "I know."

Grrl is still growling, a steady warning sound. A volunteer pokes her head in—LaSaundra, in her BULLDOGS RULE! sweatshirt and "You doing the runs, Rachel?" she asks me, looking curiously at Griffin.

"In a minute."

"I guess I'll go, then." He puts his hand out, and pats my shoulder, an awkward pat. "See you tomorrow." On the way out, he stops once more to see the kittens; I know because I see him turn right, toward the cat room, instead of left toward the door.

Grrl growls the whole time I do the other runs, a steady ragged sound, but I try to tell myself it's normal, Griffin's a total stranger, of course she's going to react badly to a stranger. . . . I pour a little pile of Wagalongs for her to eat, but she won't touch them, just keeps watching me and growling; she looks cornered, and angry, and scared. Always scared. The other dogs smell the treats, so I have to give each of them at least one, which they eat, all of them, right from my hand, while the pile in front of Grrl's cage stays untouched.

When my work's done I get out the book I brought—

S. E. Hinton's *The Outsiders*, I have to read it anyway for Psych—and settle down to start reading aloud to her, starting where I left off: where Ponyboy and Johnny are hiding out in the church, and Ponyboy quotes a poem he likes, "Nothing gold can stay"—

—and suddenly I'm crying, no sound, just tears, looking at Grrl's dark eyes, *nothing gold can stay* and "Grrl," I whisper, "please, please be OK." See her there in the cage, street dog needing a wash, a brush, hair clumps and hot spots and one bald leg, dirty and feral, *she's not ever going to be adoptable, by you or anyone else* but oh Grrl, please Grrl, you have to learn to trust me, oh please Grrl take the Wagalongs so I can take you home.

6

aturday night, eight-thirty and I'm lying on my bed: humps of blanket and twisted sheets, three pillows, I've slept with three pillows since I was two years old. The lights are off so the room is dark beneath the midnight-blue ceiling, I painted it myself, put up those stick-on stars that are supposed to be for little kids but so what. Glow-in-the-dark constellations, Cygnus, Virgo, Ursa Major, see your future in the stars. I've got the radio on, something low and slow and chronic-sounding, dirge guitars and no drums, just like I feel.

From the kitchen I hear sounds, a muted thump and rustle, running water. My mother left an hour ago for her weekly night out, embroidery class and dinner with friends, her work friends from CAC. She'd told me she was going and what to do about dinner, like I couldn't figure it out for myself; but anyway I'm not eating, I'm not hungry. Not after what happened today.

The phone rings, two rings, Brad picks up. Then two quick

knocks on my door, thunk-thunk and he's sticking his head in, he's flicking the light on, he's looking at me like I'm a number that won't add up. "I ordered from Margarita's. Come on."

"I'm not hungry."

He frowns, like I'm not hungry just to spite him. Standing there in his neon-green exercise pants, a T-shirt that reads MY PLAY MY WAY, his expensive new sneakers, you wouldn't believe how much he spends on sneakers. Like wearing them's going to make him eighteen and a jockboy again. How did I wind up with a jockboy for a father? Can anything ever go right for me? "Well, I got a double order of enchiladas and Spanish rice. I'll just have to throw your half away."

I don't point out that he could just put it in Tupperware or something, or that Mom already left dinner for us, some kind of tuna thing to heat up; I don't say anything, I just lie there, staring at him. At least Mom would ask what's wrong, even if I didn't answer her. But he just walks away and leaves the door open, like he's done all his parental duty by informing me about the food.

Even the smell from the kitchen, a spicy, red-chili smell, makes me feel sick; I feel sick anyway. I have a million things to do—start the Susan Jardine book, finish my Psych reading, work on the contest essay, which is due pretty soon—but I don't want to move, or read, or write. Especially write. Especially about Grrl.

What am I going to do?

Even to think about it makes me feel sicker, it plays like a movie in my head, a weird speeded-up tragedy, picture after picture in a flashback loop. The first one's me, very early at the shelter, meeting Jake with the Newfie cage in his pickup truck. Then me and Jake inside, trying to figure out how to maneuver Grrl into the new cage, positioning it this way and that way because *We have to do this just right*, says Jake, his forehead wrinkled into deep grooves. *If she gets loose on us in here we're really going to be in trouble.*

Next picture: Grrl in the wall cage, growling louder and louder, looking back and forth between us, her gaze as trapped as she is, furious and afraid. Next picture the growl's a snarl and she's all fight, a tornado of teeth and fur, having four strong legs under her made it so much worse—

—and in the next picture we're struggling, sweating, my sweatshirt sleeve's ripped to the elbow, Jake's trying to drive her into the Newfie cage as I fight to keep the cage doors aligned and at the same time stay out of Jake's way, and Grrl's, *careful Rachel careful!* because for one long second she's got a paw out, claws scrabbling against the floor, her whole big body straining and she's *strong*, oh so much stronger than I thought she would be—

—and in the next picture there's blood, Jake's swearing and jerking away, blood all down his arm and more on Grrl, a big ugly splotch on her chest ruff, red as a wound in the dirty white fur—

—and in the next-to-last picture there's a blanket half-over the Newfie cage, one of the old van blankets, chewed up and blue, and Jake's looking at me, panting, we're both panting and I *don't know about this, kiddo*. Just like that, just *I don't know*. Which is not like Jake. Which is really bad. And I'm helping him bandage his hand, already it's swelling and I'm begging him, *Don't write* it up, please, give her a chance, you said yourself she's got an attitude, she just doesn't understand!

Rachel, you know the drill.

I do know it: it's state law. You get bit, you report it, the dog goes into rabies quarantine for ten days, period. But ten more days of Grrl shut up in a cage. . . . *Jake, just, just wait a day or two, OK? Will you just do that?*

But he doesn't say yes or no, he never said anything, I still don't know if he's going to write it up or not. Finally in the last picture he's gone, and I'm there alone, slumped on the floor and staring at Grrl; the buzz of the fluorescents, the rustling, snuffling sounds of the other dogs, just sitting there like I went through a war or something, until Melissa came and stood over me and asked, *So what's the deal with the cage?*

Jake brought it, I told her, staring up like I was at the bottom of a hole. *So we're not wasting any space on Gr— on the collie.*

She gave me a look then, a long one with narrowed eyes, until finally *We have to talk,* she said. *Come and see me after your shift.*

But I didn't, I left, I didn't want to hear what she was going to say. All the way home I made up speeches in my head, stuff that would sway her—*Grrl can change, give me more time, all I need is a safe place.* A place without other animals, without people, some place where she can take all the time she needs to learn to trust me. And once she's able to trust, even a little . . then everything, everything will change.

But what if she never does?

Now the music on the radio changes to hammering drums, a furious, fast chant—*go go on go on go on*—and I start banging my fist against the wall, banging in time, banging past the fear that sits on my heart like a dead thing, the fear that tells me *no matter what you do it won't happen it won't work*

go on go on go

"Rachel!"

it won't work and you know what happens then your fault your fault your fault

on go on

"Rachel!" and here's Brad back in the doorway, napkin crushed in hand; I can hear TV, the little TV in the kitchen turned up loud. "Turn that off, I'm trying to watch the news!"

"You're the one who left the door open."

He's half gone already, his order delivered, but turns back. "What did you say?"

"Are you deaf?" Why is he bothering me now? Can't he see I'm losing it? The rage is bubbling in my throat, greasy red bubbles like magma, it's hard to breathe in all that heat. "I *said*, you're the one who left the *door open*."

"*What?*" like he really is deaf, or stunned or something, and then in his big voice, his monster-truck voice, "You'd better watch your mouth, little girl, you don't talk to your father that way—"

"I just did. Now *leave me alone.*"

I'm staring at him upside down, fist against the wall and I feel like Grrl, like I could tear him to pieces, like I'm nothing but teeth and rage and pain, and after a minute, a long, long minute he just walks away, down the hall, back to the kitchen . . . as I reach back over my head to close the door, slam the door to make it rattle, as if I could shut out forever what happened today.

dark again; now hunger is hurting me too. i eat some little crawlers on the ground, but they are like eating nothing. hard to stay awake, on guard—

—and a car-sound, slow-rolling, stopping close by; i breathe small, very small, hearing a They come out, come close and closer to the box-building

to me

too close

AFRAID

because i can't run *i can't run*

as the They looks in the door, light-stick pointing into the dark: big male They, white and brown and "Hey," nice, nice noises like They sometimes make but no They is nice or safe, i have to *run* but i can't run so i growl, show all my teeth at the They who keeps coming

to grab hit hurt

AFRAID AFRAID AFRAID

but too hurt to even try to run so i have to fight, bite, i bite like i am only teeth but the They has a stick, a tangle of cords, the They is strong and i fall on my leg and the *hurt!* oh! like fire, i yelp and twist as the They wraps the cords on me, pulls tugs as i yelp again, over and over, but no escape, HURT now as big as AFRAID

and now a car, big car, and a little box, walls like

lines that hurt to bite. caught! caught! when will the hurt start? what will They do to me now? in this terrible car full of ones like me, and cats, and even wilder ones, raccoons i smell and possum—as the They, panting now as i pant, shuts the doors of the big car, makes it growl and makes it go.

7

Eight-fifteen; I'm late; so what. Dragging to my locker, dragging down the hall, into Psych where Mr. Hollmer's into Stress and Behavior in *The Outsiders*: "Under stress, Johnny's behavior changes. He's able to defend himself, to stand up for himself in ways he could not have achieved before."

"You call stabbing some guy an achievement?" That's Kendra, Miss Class Clown. It's too early to get a real laugh but she does get a few snickers, and looks around the room, pleased with herself.

Mr. Hollmer pretends he doesn't hear, or maybe he really doesn't, maybe he's gone selectively deaf after too many years of teaching. He looks a hundred and five, with a haircut to match, but he's probably sixty or something. Don't they make you retire when you're sixty? "Ponyboy talks about Johnny looking as if he was 'having the time of his life' in the fire, as they worked together to save the children. Now, how can stress be a positive influence on behavior?"

Who cares? I have so much stress in my life now my head's about to blow up, and it's not influencing me positively. Like my mother getting all depressed and talkative yesterday about me "arguing" with Brad: *You don't have to agree with him, Rachel, but you do have to respect him, he's your dad,* which of course is meaningless so I said, *If he does something worth respecting then I will,* which upset her even more. Which was not my object. Although sometimes I think she secretly agrees with me about him, but she can't admit it out loud. Like he's a job she can't quit because she needs the money.

But even when she was at me about Brad she was giving me the mother-bear look, inspecting the cub for damage until *What's wrong?* she wanted to know, sitting awkwardly on the edge of my bed, the hall light casting half her face in shadow. *It's not just your dad—what's wrong?*

Nothing.

If you don't want to tell me, that's your business, although she looked all dejected when she said it. *But I can see for myself that something's really wrong.*

And for a second, just a second, I wished I could tell her, tell someone, get it off my chest—now I know why people say that, as if what happened was a weight, still on top of me, slowly crushing out my breath, and if I told it would move the weight enough so I could breathe.

I didn't tell, of course; what can she do about it? Wish me luck? Pat me on the head and say, *There there?* But just for that minute I wished I could have said how scared I felt, scared and sad and I think she saw it because Oh, Rachel, she said, and put her hand on my shoulder: a warm hand, but small. I never realized before how small her hands are. *You take everything so hard, you always have. Even when you were a tiny little girl.*

Now Mr. Hollmer's looking my way and frowning, did he ask me a question or something? but "I know," Kendra says. "Dallas acts like that because he wants to act big, like he thinks he's a *real man*, right, guys?" and she rolls her eyes at some of the boys who make noises back at her, raspberry spit sounds and then the bell goes, thank God, and I head out of there, trudging down the hall to Language Arts—

—where Mrs. Cruzelle is waiting, she motions me over right away and "How's the essay coming?" she asks.

The walls are full of glossy new posters from stage productions like *Macbeth* and *King Lear* and *The Merchant of Venice*: people in wigs and costumes, people in masks, I feel like I'm wearing a mask now as I shrug, and look down at her desk; I don't know what to say. I don't want to tell her I can't work on it because I'm so stressed about Grrl, the real Grrl, there in the cage with time running out. I don't want to tell her that right now I don't even care about the stupid contest, that going to State in the summer seems as distant, and as likely, as going to the moon. And even if I did win, and did go, what would happen to Grrl then?

But I don't want to say those things, not to her. Yet I don't want to lie, either, make a happy face even if I could, so "Not too good," I say, and look away—

—to see Griffin ambling in the door, today he's wearing a

Super Chicken T-shirt, you know Super Chicken? It's this dumb cartoon from a long time ago, they show it on cable. In fact it's so dumb it cheers me up, especially when he sees me looking and makes chicken wings, you know, like flapping his elbows and "Cluck cluck," he says to me in passing, going to his seat; he has a new seat now, next to mine, in the back. "Cluck cluck—"

"Well, that's about right," Chelsea says to Jon; she's wearing a tight skirt and her legs are crossed, and she's swinging one foot back and forth, back and forth. "He's a chicken and she's a dog."

"He's a chicken all right. You should see him in gym," says Jon, and laughs, and Chelsea laughs, and Courtney laughs but the only face I see is Griffin's: as it closes, shuts down like, a time-lapse picture, eyes, mouth, everything going dead and "You should see yourself," I say to Jon. I can feel my own face turning red, my heart is pounding like a drum, war drum. "See what a shallow shitty creepy—"

"Shut up, Rachel, you loser bitch—"

—and that's when Griffin grabs at him, more of a shove than anything else but he lunges over the desk to do it so they both fall backwards in a crash of desks and before they can get up Mrs. Cruzelle's there between them, saying, "Stop it right now! Griffin, Jon—"

—and then the hall monitor comes in, pushing through the circle, pulling at Griffin and Jon and "She started it," Chelsea's yelling at Mrs. Cruzelle and "Both of them," says Mrs. Cruzelle to the hall monitor; she doesn't look at me. "Rachel and Chelsea, you too."

So off we go, the monitor escorting us like prisoners to the Dean of Students' waiting room. Plastic chairs, a yellowing, half-dead fern, lots of motivational posters on the wall: BELIEVE = ACHIEVE with a picture of a sailboat in a sunset, and DO THE RIGHT THING!! which is what I just did but here I am anyway. Griffin sits staring down at his shoes; he doesn't say anything to me. Jon and Courtney mutter back and forth to one another and when the secretary's not looking Jon flips me off. He seems to have a limited range of insults.

First the monitor goes in, then when she comes out there's Mr. James standing in the doorway. He's really tall and totally bald and has a kind of liquid accent, like he comes from the South but he's working on it. "Ms. Thayne? Mr. Truman?" he says; he always calls people Mr. and Ms. "Come on in."

Why them first, and not us? and "Oh great," I say, mostly to myself and the posters since the secretary's on the phone and Griffin seems to be in another world, he hasn't looked at me once but "Cleanup," he says to me now, under his breath, and I see that he's smiling, a very very small smile, like he's almost enjoying himself. "It's always better to bat cleanup . . . to go last," when he sees I don't know what he means. "Don't worry. When I was at Burgess—"

"I'm not worried. I'm mad."

"Listen," he says, leaning forward: now he's really smiling, like we're not here, like we're out on the steps or something. "I was going to tell you in class before all this started happening, but— Anyway. I had a great idea. About your dog."

"What?"

"Your dog," impatient. "You need a place to take her, right? To get her out of the shelter? Well, I—"

—and of course the door opens right then and "Mr. Gunn,"

says Mr. James. "Ms. Hawthorne. . . . Wait out here, Ms. Thayne, Mr. Truman."

The inner office has more posters—PERSEVERANCE, with a bunch of mountain climbers on Everest or something—but the chairs are nicer and the plant's alive. Mr. James doesn't say anything as we sit down, he doesn't say anything as we wait, maybe he's never going to say anything . . . until finally "Sticks and stones," he says. "Ms. Hawthorne, did you say that Jon Truman was"—he looks at a notepad— "a 'shallow, shitty creep'?"

"No. I said he was shallow *and* shitty *and* creepy."

"He called her names, too," Griffin says in a conversational kind of way, like we're all just sitting here chatting. He's not upset, or even mad like me; does he *like* being here? *When I was at Burgess . . .* was he a troublemaker or something? Lost Boys aren't usually, they're more like the monkey wrench in the gears, what Mr. Hollmer in Psych calls passive-aggressive.

"Mr. Gunn, I'm getting to you. —What prompted this character assessment, Ms. Hawthorne?"

All of a sudden it all sounds so dumb, the whole thing—*he's a chicken and she's a dog, shallow and shitty*—like we're in kindergarten or something, spitting in each other's milk. And it doesn't even get near the real problem, which is that they think they're so much better than us that we're not even in the same species, they think they rule this school by divine right and I think they should go to hell and take the school with them. Except for Mrs. Cruzelle. Poor Mrs. Cruzelle, the referee. So "They called us names and then I called him a name and then Griffin shoved him and they fell over the desk. Nobody hit anybody. And that's all that happened."

"Is that right, Mr. Gunn?"

Griffin shrugs and picks at his thumb. "That's right. Except that Truman called Rachel a name afterward, too."

"I don't care," I say. "I don't care what Jon Truman—"

"Ms. Hawthorne, Mr. Gunn is talking now. What did he say, Mr. Gunn?"

Griffin stops picking his thumb and sits straighter; he looks Mr. James in the face for the first time. "He said, he said she was a loser bitch. I bet he didn't tell you that part, did he?"

Mr. James makes a little note on his pad. "And then you hit him?"

"I shoved him," looking down again, as if he's sorry he hadn't hit Jon—but I'm glad he didn't, that's an immediate suspension, no questions asked. They're really paranoid about fighting here, and safety; I guess they have to be.

"I see," says Mr. James. He makes a few more notes, then goes to the door to call in Chelsea and Jon and "I'll keep this brief," he says, looking at each of us in turn. "No one here is a creep, or a loser, unless he or she chooses to be. *You are what you want to be.*"

No one says anything. I see Jon trying to catch Griffin's eye, Mr. James must see it too because "This incident stops here," he says, both hands on his desk, thumping a little to get the point across. "If it continues, in the hallways, at lunch, outside of school—I'll hear about it. And I'll take appropriate action." He looks at all of us, but hardest at Jon, who won't meet his gaze.

"You're almost adults," he says. "Act like it. Ms. Hawthorne, Ms. Thayne, you can go. Mr. Gunn, Mr. Truman, you have a detention hour, starting now."

Out in the hall, I don't look at Chelsea, just walk down the hall on the other side: as if I'm in a different school, on a different planet, which I am. Back in class everyone stares as we walk in, everyone but Mrs. Cruzelle who keeps on talking about whatever she's talking about, I can't concentrate and I don't even try, just sit waiting for the bell but "Rachel," she says as I pass her desk. "I need to talk with you, can you stop by at lunch?"

Lunch? but that's when I'll see Griffin, and find out about his great idea *about your dog* . . . but Mrs. Cruzelle looks so, so—what? I don't know, I can't name it but it's not good so "OK," I say reluctantly. "I'll be there."

When I get there she's alone, piling up some papers, she stops when she sees me and "Come on in," she says. "Mr. James was just here."

Oh great, now what? but she smiles a little: "No, no, it's nothing bad. In fact he had some nice things to say about you, he said you're a very articulate young person. Which you are," which means she's leading into the essay, which means I have to say something about it, but what can I say? without lying?

So with one eye on the clock—because I *have* to find Griffin— I try to sound all positive, which I'm not very good at: like I'll have it done soon, no problem and maybe I even will, maybe Griffin's great idea really will be great and we can somehow get her out of there, and she'll learn to trust me, and I can write a big wild juicy happy ending—but "Rachel," Mrs. Cruzelle says quietly, then pauses, one of her trademark pauses, until she's sure I'm listening.

"You know," she says, "this world"—sweeping one arm back and forth, to take in the room, the school, all of it—"is a small place. Some people need a bigger world. Like you. And Susan

Jardine knows a lot of people, people who run workshops, and fiction programs at universities—her class could be the door into that bigger world. And your writing talent is the key to that door. But you have to use the key."

I don't say anything, because she's right: about the world, and Susan Jardine, and writing. From the hall outside I hear voices, laughing, locker sounds; small-world sounds. School is just a small world, I guess, like a shirt you've outgrown but you still have to wear for a while. But the stuff she's talking about, Susan Jardine and universities and all that, seems so indistinct and far away, like a place on the horizon that I might or might not reach someday. Here, right here in front of me, is finding Griffin, finding out about his idea, and saving Grrl. I don't want to sacrifice one for the other, but I don't know how to balance what only might happen with what's really happening right now.

So I sit silent for a minute, a long minute. Finally "I have a lot going on in my life right now," I say, which sounds lame, but I can't help that. "But I'll do my best to get the essay done."

She nods, a little sadly; doesn't she believe me? and "If you want me to review it later," she says, "I'll be glad to. But I won't ask you about it anymore."

Without meaning to I look past her, to the clock on the wall, 12:18 already and "Better get some lunch," she says, and picks up her papers again. "I'll see you tomorrow."

It seems like I should say something else, but what? Something, something better that I don't know so I just head out, hurrying down the hall to the Media Center—but no Griffin there. So I check the steps, then the cafeteria (where Chelsea, Courtney, Jon, and their clique start barking as soon as they see me, oh grow *up*), then the Media Center again, where can he be? looking for me? You have a better chance of finding someone if one of you stays put, so it's back to the steps where I wait, and check my watch, and check my watch, until lunch is over and "Shit!" I snarl and storm into school—

—and there he is, heading for the stairs, head down, but when I call his name—when I yell his name—he jerks up and around and "Where were you?" I say, wading through Walla-Wallas. "I looked everywhere—"

"I was looking for you! —Here," and he pushes something into my hand, a little scrap of paper, a phone number and "Call me," he says. "I have to make up Cruzelle's class after school, so I'll be late. But when you come over, we'll start."

"Start what? Where?"

"The dog pen," he says. "At my house."

8

Ever since he told me I've been jumping up and down, inside I mean. It's like I can't believe what's happening: we're going to take Grrl to Griffin's house! His parents—or his mom, I guess—don't care, and Grrl can have everything she needs: lots of room, and privacy, and no other animals, and only Griffin and me to take care of her until she calms down and learns to trust, however long it takes.

Oh, this is going to work. I know it is.

His house—I see, wheeling up in the driveway—is nothing like mine. It's lots bigger, for one thing, and it's old, the stately, expensive kind of old: red brick and lots of ivy, the stuff that's so thick you could climb it. I can't see in back, there's a privacy fence, but you can tell the yard is big. Perfect for a dog who needs her space.

Griffin answers the door so fast it's as if he was waiting behind it. Inside is a wall of books, long wooden bookcases like in a library and "Wow," I say, checking some of the authors—

Salinger, Sylvia Plath, Susan Jardine!—"this is great. At my house the library is *Time* magazine."

Griffin laughs. He's different here somehow, he moves faster, he talks louder and talks more: like now, as he leads me into the kitchen, "You want a soda or something? or iced tea?" and in the same breath "You should have seen Truman in detention," taking a bag of chips from the cupboard, banging the door shut with his elbow. "He didn't know what to do with himself for an hour, I felt like giving him a coloring book or something to take the edge off."

"Hello," someone says from behind us: it's Griffin's mom. Short dark hair, loose white sweater, her eyes are gray like his—but very calm, like lake water, a deep lake quiet and still. "I'm Anna Gunn. You must be Rachel," and she shakes my hand, which is weird but kind of nice, one adult to another. "Griffin's told me a little about the dog. She sounds beautiful."

"She is beautiful."

"When Griffin said a girl was coming to stay with us, I thought for a minute he was talking about a girlfriend, but—"

"Mom, *God*."

"—I guess that's the dog's name? Girl?" and I smile and nod as "Come on," Griffin says to me, heading down the hall and "I got some blueprints from online," he says as he climbs the stairs; his voice sounds different now, muted, I can tell he's embarrassed by the girlfriend thing. I am too, a little, I mean I guess that's the first thing people would think about us, a guy and a girl hanging out together, but I never thought it . . . did Griffin? No. Did he? and "In here," he says. "Look out for all the junk."

You know, I thought my room was messy, but this is like an

order of magnitude worse. But it's not as if it's dirty, like smelly or moldy with old food or gruesome socks. It's more like a bird's nest: here's a twig and here's some fluff and here's some straw, but instead it's clothes and magazines and CDs and "Here," he says, pulling out some papers from the middle of the mess. "Take a look at these. . . . You can sit on the bed if you want. If you can find it."

Under some T-shirts there's a beanbag chair, so I sit on that. The room's windows face west, big windows, he's got them mostly covered but now he pulls up the blinds so I can read.

The stuff's from a Humane Society site, a whole how-to: *Doghouses should be made of wood or plastic; metal conducts cold. Car doormats may be used to shelter the door. Use straw as bedding, never rugs or blankets that can get wet or freeze.* And then there are plans for building pens, how much lumber, how to measure and "I don't have a lot of tools," he says, "but it doesn't look like we'll need a lot. Saturday's supposed to be nice, we can start then if you want."

Build the house Saturday, then get started on the pen—or should we do the pen first? And get supplies, straw and food and bowls—and a leash, and a muzzle, I usually don't like muzzles but in this case. . . . I have to tell Jake, and Melissa, right away, tomorrow when I go in, maybe Jake can help us move her here? and "It'll be OK, right?" Griffin asks, tentatively. "I mean, she's wild, but she'll calm down, right?"

"Sure." She has to. "She just needs time."

I flip through the blueprints, wondering what kinds of tools might be in our garage, maybe Brad has some and "You ever have a dog?" Griffin asks.

I think of Sassy, the Kaisers' poodle. "No. Not really."

"Me neither." He doesn't say anything for a while and neither do I, but it's not an awkward silence; it's—nice. Just nice. His eyes are closed now, and when he talks it's like he's thinking out loud: "This is going to be so ten."

"So what?"

His eyes open. "Nothing. It's—ten," when he sees I'm not going to let it go. "Like on a scale of one to ten, you know? It's something I used to say, it's just a stupid—"

"No it's not. It *is* going to be ten. Maybe eleven," and we both laugh, not because it's funny but because we feel like laughing, because we feel . . . happy. And then "Did your mom," I ask, because I have to ask, "did she really think I was your girlfriend? And that I was going to, to live here?"

"She's so weird. Don't pay any attention to her."

"No, she's OK." It's like everybody thinks their families are the worst people on earth, but mostly they're all just normal. Except for Brad. And sometimes my mother.

"I mean, not that it would be, be bad, or something." Now he's blushing, like he did with the kittens, a warm, bright flush. "I mean, to think that."

I open my mouth, then shut it; his face keeps getting redder. Finally "I never had a boyfriend," I say, which is not what I meant to say, but now that it's out I'm glad. "Or a, a best friend, either. When I was little"—sitting out in the yard, by the honey-suckle vines— "I used to wonder how people could be friends, I mean how did it happen? Like I knew kids, from school, and from my street, but I never—I just, didn't like what they liked, and they didn't like what I liked, so—"

"Or they thought you were a geek," he says, "for liking what you liked. Or for not playing sports. . . . I *hate* sports. Everything but tennis. Which is not a big macho thing to play."

Sun pours through the window, warming the room like a safe little cave, like I feel warmed inside; I've never really talked to anyone this way, I've never been able to say things like "I used to hate them," I say, "but, but I wanted to *be* them, too. Be part of it. Whatever 'it' was."

"Or even just get them off your back. It's like, every school I went to was the same school—Price, and Kennedy, and Roger Day, and Burgess, always the same deal, always the same bull-shit." The blush is gone from his face; now he looks tired, and older somehow, as if he'd had something proved to him he didn't want to know. "There're a lot of Trumans in this world, you know?"

"I know." I shift on the beanbag chair, let the sun touch my face. "Once I tried to explain to my mother, when she wanted me to go play with the girl across the street—this girl was an idiot, she used to spit in people's milk—anyway, I told my mom that this girl and I were like magnets, pushing against each other, repelling each other, you know?"

"And she looked at you like you were crazy, right?"

"Yes! Like she was worried before that I didn't want to play, but now she was even *more* worried, that I was an alien or some-thing." I laugh, now, but I wasn't laughing then. Then I felt . . . I don't know, like, frozen inside, and—and ashamed, like my own mother thought I was weird, so I must *be* weird. "So after that I gave up trying to explain, and just did what I wanted to do."

Griffin nods. "When I lived with my dad he was always trying

72

to get me to play baseball with him. I mean, thanks but no thanks, OK? Although he did buy me a new racquet for Christmas last year."

"Do you see your dad a lot?"

"When I want to." He reaches for his soda. "Sometimes I stay with him, in the summer, you know?"

"I might go away this summer," I say, and tell him about the essay contest, about Susan Jardine and "It's a master class," I say, "at State." The sun has moved, is in my eyes, so I shift, scoot the bag a little closer to Griffin. "It sounds cool. . . . So Mrs. Cruzelle's on my back about that essay, to get it done and send it in."

"Well, it's really good," he says, frowning a little, as if he's just thought of something he doesn't like; what? Then he smiles again and "I know how it ends," he says. "Your essay. Happily ever after, in my back yard."

We talk some more about Saturday, as the sun drifts lower, slow gold going down, I have to go too so "I'll call you," I say as we walk downstairs, "after I talk to Jake. And Melissa." I imagine their faces, their surprise and *See?* I'll say. *See, I told you, I knew I could save her* and "You know," I say to Griffin at the door, "this is really nice, what you're doing. *Really* nice."

"Well, no one here's allergic or anything, and I thought . . . I just wanted to help. Help your dog."

"When she gets here," I say, "she'll be our dog." It feels a little funny to say it, to share her, but he deserves it. And the look he gives me then, I can't describe it, but I feel it, all the way to my heart. It feels—

"*Eleven*," he says; his eyes are shining, clear and gray. "Pure eleven."

"At least," I say; I'm smiling too, a smile that fills my whole face. "See you tomorrow."

I see him watching as I coast down the driveway; I give him a big backwards wave, and he waves back. Riding home, I feel like I'm floating, like I hardly have to touch the pedals, like I could ride right into the golden heart of the sun. Eleven; I feel pure eleven.

Gliding up to the garage I see my mother's van but not the Jeep. Inside the rich scent of soup, her homemade tomato-basil soup, of baking bread and "Hi," she says; she looks tired, like always, but she smiles. "Dinner's just about ready."

"I'll set the table."

The bread is pumpkin-wheat, my favorite. She turns on the radio, the classical station: silver sounds, violins and flutes and "How was the shelter?" she asks, ladling soup into deep blue bowls. Ordinarily I would have said *fine* and let it go, but today isn't an ordinary day, today is today so I tell her I wasn't at the shelter, I was at a friend's house. Which surprises her, I can see, because as far as she knows I don't have any friends. But she doesn't press me, or ask any questions, just says "Oh?" and keeps eating soup. Which kind of surprises me.

Violin and cello now, the fading heat of the oven; outside it's full dusk, a charcoal-gray and blue and "I love this time of day," she says. "The sky is just tremendous. . . . You know, the school called earlier. A Mr. James."

Oh great. What's it going to be? a Q&A? a lecture? but instead

"He told me what happened," she says, still spooning her soup, "and I told him I thought you'd handled yourself pretty well, all things considered." Surprise number two. Plus she's smiling, just a little, just at the corners of her mouth. "I did tell him I'd speak to you about appropriate language—"

"I know, I know, you're not supposed to swear in—"

"—and now I have, so we don't have to talk about it anymore." She butters some bread. "Sometimes I swear at work, which isn't exactly appropriate either. But Maria Elena hogs the fax machine, I mean every day at four-thirty, like clockwork—" and she goes into a little tale about Maria Elena, whoever she is, and Jerry Somebody and Lucie Somebody Else and then dinner's over and "Is Griffin the one?" she asks, brushing crumbs off the table; I carry the plates to the sink. "That you were visiting, I mean?"

"Yeah."

"Mr. James said he stuck up for you. He sounds like a good friend to have."

I think of Grrl, *our dog.* "He is."

"I'm glad." She starts filling the sink. "One good friend can make up for a lot." And she smiles at me over her shoulder, the way Griffin's mother shook my hand: like one adult to another, one *person* to another. It feels weird again, but good, and even better when I smile back.

Is it possible that I'm having a perfect day?

In my room I turn the dimmer switch down, the radio on, and burrow through the crap in my backpack: I need to finish *The Outsiders* for Psych, do a math sheet, blah blah blah . . . but first I mash up my pillows, pull out my notebook, and get back to work on the essay. *Happily ever after* because this is going to work, I know it, she'll never have a better chance than this.

at first i only sleep. like water, deep and dark, i wake and struggle and go down again. AFRAID is in the darkness, AFRAID never leaves, but this sleep is stronger even than AFRAID.

many here are like me: big ones, small ones, all caught in the small boxes made with hard lines. i smell cats, too, and They, many many They, in and out and making nice sounds, but all i do is growl. AFRAID waits, buzzing in my head like bees; to bite the lines is no good and hurts my teeth so i don't try anymore. just growl, and smell, and wait.

my leg now not so hurt, wrapped warm and white in strange flat fur, i don't reach the bite when i lick, i can't pull the strange fur off. there is water here, clean water so no more thirst, i drink as much as i want and then more comes. food too, They bring it but i never eat while They watch, only growl, growl until they go, then eat as fast as i can.

a They comes all the time to me, a young They i think, more nice noises, like nice growling: *grrl. grrl.* this They brings different food, strange small chunks like meat but not meat, i eat them later and wish for more.

then the young They and the car They come; AFRAID comes with them; what is happening now? is now the time for hurt? the small box opens, can i run? —and i try, oh! try hard to get away, claws digging down but nowhere to dig, teeth bare to bite

bite

—and "ow" from the car They, some kind of bark, drag push pull into another box, bigger but still hard lines, still i can't run. blood on my fur, i smell it; not my blood.

now they bark at each other, They and They, the young They is very loud. i growl until They go, then wait: for the box to open, for room to run away.

9

*I*t's hard for me to write sad when I'm so happy, when I'm all adrenaline, but I have to be true to the story. So "Here's what I've got so far," I say to Mrs. Cruzelle, handing her the new pages; I got to school early so I could print them out in the Media Center. "It's still not done, but I'm getting closer."

"Terrific." Today she's wearing a pair of dog earrings, pewter dogs dangling, they don't really make it as a fashion statement but a dog is a dog and "I like your earrings," I say.

"Well thank you. I got them at a breeders' show." People are starting to come in; not Griffin yet, though. "You can't really tell, but they're supposed to be Airedales. . . . I used to breed them, but now I have just the two. Jack and Jill. They're enough."

Chelsea and Courtney pass by the desk, wearing identical white long-sleeve shirts; they don't look at me, and I don't look at them. That's the way it's been in here, with Jon Truman too. If they see me anywhere else they still bark, you'd think they'd be tired of it by now but you'd be wrong. Small minds are very easily amused.

"Why'd you stop?" I ask Mrs. Cruzelle. "Breeding them, I mean?"

"I don't have the energy anymore. It takes a lot, to work with big dogs. You know that. . . . Bailey, can you come up here? —I'll read this on my planning hour," she says to me, tucking the pages away. "Stop by after school if you want."

I do want, I mean I'd like to, but today's The Day so "I can't today," I say and here comes Griffin, giving me the V-for-victory sign and "I couldn't sleep," I murmur as we sit down. "I just sat up all night thinking. And I wrote some more pages."

"I couldn't sleep either. I kept hearing dogs bark."

Class seems long; lunch seems long; the day seems longer than it ever has before. Griffin's as antsy as a two-year-old, and when Chelsea and her clique start up the barking in the lunch line he barks back. It makes me laugh, a laugh like effervescence, like breathlessness and "Two more hours," I say, checking my watch.

"One hour and fifty-eight minutes. Will you call me, as soon as you get home?"

"As soon."

"Eleven."

"Twelve!"

Finally it's three, we're out, I'm gone and "Call me!" Griffin shouts as I ride away, I took my bike so I could leave straight from school. Did I ever ride faster? I feel like I'm flying, I'm there in less than twenty minutes and "Hey," says LaSaundra as I walk in; she gives me a funny look. "You OK?"

Am I OK? What kind of question is that? and "I'm fine," I say. "Melissa in her office?"

"Yeah." And she gives me another weird look, what is it, is my head on backwards or something? In the hall I hear Melissa's voice, she's on the phone so I decide to check first on Grrl, give her the good news, not that she can understand it but she will, she will—

—and "Grrl," I call as I step into the dog room, all the dogs barking when they see me, this kind of barking I like. "Hey guys, hey babies . . . Grrl," to the Newfie cage with its blanket drape, no growl from inside, is she sleeping? "Grrl?"

I lift the blanket. She's not there.

"Grrl?" I say to the empty cage, who moved her? and why? and "Grrl," again and louder, checking cage after cage: she's not in this room, or the holding room, where is she? and "Grrl!" out into the hall, rushing past LaSaundra who stands there with a handful of leashes, and when she looks at me again I know.

Grrl's dead.

And right away "Rachel," sharp from behind me, it's Melissa. "Rachel, my office, now. Now," hard, her hand on my arm but I shake her off, my whole body is shaking and when my voice comes out it sounds like someone screaming. "She's dead! You killed her!"

"Listen to me," Melissa says, loud, right into my face like a person yelling into the wind. "She bit Karen yesterday, a bad bite—and Jake, too, I found out about Jake—"

"*You killed her!*" and now I am screaming, people are rushing into the hall, saying things to me, but all I hear is barking and the sound of the blood in my head, my heart beating faster and faster and "You killed my dog," from inside that sound; am I still screaming? I don't know.

"Do you think I wanted to? I—*listen* to me, I had no choice! Ten more days in a cage, you think she's wild now—and then to be put down anyway—"

"She wasn't going to be put down! We had a place, we were going to keep her—"

"Keep her how? In a cage, forever? I never should have let you do this in the first place. It was cruel to her, it—"

"You're the one who's cruel! You're the one who killed her behind my back, you waited till I wasn't here—"

"That's not true! Jake called you this morning, but your mother said you'd left for school already. —I told him not to, I knew you would act this way—"

and all of a sudden I'm not there anymore, not in that hallway closing in on me, my head is closing in on me, driving me onto a point so black and so sharp I can feel it even before it touches me and the point is *pain*, the point is Grrl with a needle in her leg, Grrl dying alone and afraid and

Jake called you this morning

but I wasn't there I was at school thinking today's the day

and it was but not like I thought because while I was happy she was lying there dying

dying all alone

and I'm in Melissa's office, I don't know how I got here, the door is closed and I'm in a whirlwind, papers phone the keyboard everything's falling and smashing and

"Rachel! It's Jake, Rachel, open the door—" and "Stop it! stop it!" Melissa's yelling, and that's when the computer goes, *wham!*

on the floor, everything's falling and I'm yanking at the door, out into the hall where I see faces—Jake's, Melissa's all red, LaSaundra's and Grandma Katie's—like a kaleidoscope, a funhouse-mirror blur through the tears, hot tears like napalm burning my face and now I'm running, out of the building, away, away

I have to run

until I can't anymore, I can't see, I can't breathe, I have to stop where I am which is on a sidewalk in front of a store, Windows'n'More, some guy's staring out at me but he looks away as soon as I see him; I must look crazy or something. . . . I am crazy. I'm wild, I'm feral, I'm a ghost, the ghost of Grrl. On the steel table, holding her down—

"Hey, uh, are you OK? Do you—"

The Windows'n'More guy is peering from around the door, but "No," I say, "I don't," because what can he do for me? What can anyone do? She's dead, she's gone—so I start walking again, wiping my face with my hands, the black point wedged deep in me now like a thorn, a bright steel thorn, a cold steel needle in a dog's hind leg.

You can walk a long way when you don't want to stop. Past stores and gas stations and strip malls and used-car lots, laundromats and fast-food places, the money I have with me will barely buy a chocolate shake but the lady behind the counter gives me fries for free: "Just take 'em," she says, and I do, even though I'm not really hungry, take them outside to sit on the low brick wall around the parking lot, back by the dumpster, *the big square metal thing They dump food in*—and I'm crying again, you would think I'd be all out of tears but I'm not. They come in slow rivers, burning my eyes, hot on my cold skin; I'm cold all over. The sun went down a long time ago; the lights in the parking lot are greenish-white.

Hopping off the wall, walking again, trying not to think . . . but I can't not think: of Grrl on the table, terrified, trying to get away—of Jake calling me—of me in the Media Center printing out my stupid pages, oh Grrl I'm so sorry I wasn't there, sorry *sorry*—but sorry doesn't cut it, sorry won't bring her back, sorry is out here walking until my legs feel like they're going to fall off, my hands are so cold I can't bend my fingers anymore. But there's nowhere to rest but a gas station on one corner and a Coney Island place that's closed on the other. And a bar. Where am I, anyway?

I don't have a watch on but it's late, I know, maybe midnight, and I can't keep walking around like a zombie. I don't want to go back but I have to, I can't stay here—and then: *Griffin*, I think, *I'll go to Griffin's*—

—and then I think of Griffin, happy on the sidewalk outside of school, *Call me!* and I start crying again, crying and walking, heading in the dark to Griffin's house.

How long does it take? I don't know. I can't feel time pass anymore, I'm just walking, one foot in front of the other. And after a while I know I'm getting close, almost to his street, when I see someone up ahead, hands in pockets, moving like a ghost—

—and I make a sound, I must have because he stops, he turns, it's Griffin and I see him see me, his body gets still, tall and *"Rachel!"* as he turns, sprinting toward me in the dark—

—and in ten steps he's there, reaching for me as I reach for him, like two survivors in a drowning world, the whole world drowning in tears and "She's gone," I say, through my own tears; my voice sounds strange, clogged and wet and heavy as lead. "She's dead."

"I know." His arms are shaking, I can feel them; his hands are colder than mine. He's not even wearing a jacket. "When you didn't call I knew something was wrong, so I called over there, and when I said I was your friend, they told me, they—"

"They killed her. This morning, while we were at school."

"I know." He doesn't say anything else for a minute. A siren starts up, then dies away; something—a cat—rustles by in the bushes. "And then I didn't know where you were, or what I should do. . . . Then my mom called your mom—"

"What'd she do that for?"

"I don't know." We're walking now, arms around each other's shoulders, like wounded soldiers off a battlefield. "But I guess your mom went driving around, looking for you. Where'd you go? Where were you?"

"Nowhere." Now I see his house ahead, lights on, and in the driveway a blue van, my mother's van and "Nowhere," I say again, as together we climb the porch, as we walk into the living room to see my parents waiting there.

10

"We're not pressing charges or anything," Melissa says; she stares at my mom and Brad, but she won't look at me. How many times have I been in this office? And now it feels like nowhere, like everyplace, anyplace else. "But we can't afford to replace the computer Rachel trashed—"

"I understand," says Brad. He's trying to sound nice, or concerned, or something, but mostly he just sounds incredibly pissed off: at me, at Melissa, at having to be there and not at work, where it's safe and tidy with no screaming or broken stuff. "I'll write you a check."

"Ordinarily I'd let her work it off," Melissa says, still not looking at me. "But seeing the way things are, I think it's better for everyone if she doesn't volunteer here anymore."

"You don't have to call me 'she,'" I say, looking at her: a stranger's face, wide eyes, her forehead knotted. "And I wouldn't work here again if you begged me to, I—"

"Be quiet," Brad says to me; his face is as tight as a fist. "No one's interested in what you have to say. —Do I make the check out to Brookdale Shelter?" as someone knocks, pokes his head around the door: it's Jake. "Can I see you for a minute?" he says, and it takes me a second to understand that he's talking to me.

Outside, in the hallway, he puts his hand on my shoulder, brief and warm, the other hand's still bandaged and "Hey," he says. "How're you doing, kiddo?"

I don't want to talk to Jake, if I do I'll cry—and I refuse to cry here, so I just shake my head, staring down at the floor's scuff and crud, muddy dog prints and "Don't beat yourself up," he says, very quietly. "You did the best you could for her," but that's not true, is it? If I did my best then why is she dead?—as the door opens, they're all coming out so I head to the car, hunch in the back, ignore Brad's blah blah blah about the check, it figures all he'd care about is the money but all of a sudden "Stop it," my mother says; her face is strained and blotchy, she's got her inhaler in her hand. "Just stop talking about the money, can't you see she's upset?"

"She ought to be upset. She ought to pay back what she—"

"Stop it! Just stop!" and then she starts coughing, a tight, wheezy, allergy cough, it seems to go on and on so he doesn't say anything else, no one says anything until we get home. Brad goes inside as my mother holds me back, the sun too bright in my eyes and "Rachel," she says; her voice sounds all strangly, but at least she's not coughing anymore. "What you did was wrong. But I'm so sorry about your dog, honey."

Sorry: like a little bell, sor-ry and "Why didn't you tell me?" I say. "That Jake called, why didn't you call me at school or something?" I'm looking at her in the dazzle of the sun as if she's far away, at the wrong end of the telescope, a tiny bewildered red face and "I didn't know," she finally says. "I just, I told him that you'd be in to work later, you had it on your calendar—"

"You should have called me at school." Thinking of Grrl on the table, the black thorn bright in my side, my voice gets louder and "It was *important*, it—"

"But Rachel, I didn't know it was important! You never told me about your dog—"

And then Brad's on the porch again, car keys in hand and "You need a ride to school?" he says to me, in what for him is a nice voice; school? I look at my watch, it's noon. Noon on a day like any other day, except it's not and never will be. "It's on my way, I can drop you off."

School, home, what's the difference? I'm still on the wrong side of the telescope, like life's here and I'm there . . . So I go, dragging in to Mrs. Cruzelle's, where she sits having lunch, cafeteria coffee, a cheese sandwich and "Here," I say, reaching into my backpack, pulling out *On the Matter of My Suicide*. "Here's your book back."

She looks up at me; it takes her a long minute to say anything. Then, finally, quietly: "Did you read it?"

"No."

"What about the essay?" she says, as if she already knows the answer.

"I'm not doing the essay."

"Why not?"

Because my dog is dead, my *dog* is *dead* and "I'm just not," I say, looking past her at the posters on the wall. "Get someone else to do it."

"Rachel," she says, then again, more urgently, "*Rachel*," until I look at her, look her in the eyes and "Don't cut that part of yourself off," she says. "Let it help you, now, when you really need it—"

"I don't care about the stupid contest!" The real world is getting closer, *here* and *there* starting to touch; my voice is getting louder. "I don't care about Susan Jardine or my stupid writing, OK?" because I can't write about Grrl anymore, I *can't*—and I can't talk about it either, not with her or anyone else so I hurry into the hall, into the river of Walla-Wallas that carries me along, back to my locker where "*Hey*," with relief, Griffin's there with something in his hand, a folded-up note with RACHEL on the front. "I was just going to stick it in your locker. . . . Where were you this morning?"

"At the shelter." Real life is breathing in my face now, real life is wearing a Super Chicken T-shirt, real life is the black thorn digging deeper every time I breathe so "I can't talk now," I say, "I have to go—" Go where? to the girls' bathroom? to the stairs outside? back home to my room? but "Can you come over, after school?" as he follows me down the hall. "We can look at the plans again, and—"

"Look at the *plans*?" I stop as if he's hit me. "For what? Grrl's *gone*, she's—"

"I know," with his hand on my arm. "But we can still make the pen, can't we? We can still—"

"Are you crazy? Make it for what?" The thorn's in my throat now, I can hear it in my voice. "Griffin, my dog is *dead*."

People push past us, I don't see them except as shadows, waves of motion beside him, face pale under paler hair and "I thought—" and he stops; I can see the hurt in his eyes. "I thought you said she was our dog."

I don't say anything, I can't, I start walking away but "Wait," one hand on my arm to stop me, forcing himself through the hurt. "Even if she's gone—*especially* since she's gone, we still have to help—we could get another dog, or, or those kittens. . . . I thought you *wanted* to help, that's why you worked there in the first place. Like the starfish—"

"Most of them died," I say, as the thorn digs in, digs deep, digs a hole in my heart, a hole like a grave and now I'm yelling, yelling in his face: "The whole beach was full of dead starfish, remember? The whole *beach*—"

—and he's staring at me like I'm a stranger, someone he doesn't know and doesn't want to, someone bad and "So it's all bullshit, then, right?" in a voice I never heard from him, a deep, dry voice like a desert, a wasteland voice. "You care until it really hurts, and then you stop, right?" as the bell goes, a long, flat tone and he turns away, shoulders down, worse than a Lost Boy, a ghost boy gone into the desert—

—and I'm gone too, down the emptying hall, people flowing into rooms like water down a dozen drains and "Hey," says the hall monitor as I rush by, "hey, wait a—" but I'm hitting the crashbar, I'm out the door, I'm running down the street like the building's on fire, until I can't run anymore and I have to stop, gasping, arms wrapped around me, my back pressed hard against the gray brick of a building, what is it? JOHN DENYARS, DENTIST. A lady and a little kid come out and see me, and the kid asks a question, high little voice, "Mommy, what's wrong with her?" but the mother doesn't answer, just jerks the kid along like a dog on a leash. Jake once told me you could tell everything you needed to know about people by the way they treat kids and animals. What does Jake think of me now?

And then I start walking, just walking, no destination in mind; I just need to move. One step, two steps, infinity, isn't that a game kids play? My feet hurt; my poor hightops are falling apart. . . . And every step I take seems like a thought, one thought to the other like steppingstones, hard stones in a cold, dark river—

be careful, Rachel—she's wild

keep her how? in a cage, forever?

Jake called you

I didn't know it was important, you never told me

you care until it really hurts and then you stop, right?

—and they're right, they're all right, it's all my fault. . . . Why didn't I get her out sooner, before she could bite anyone? Why didn't I tell my mother, just in case someone called? Why did I let Griffin in, then slam the door in his face?

Walking hard, stone to stone to stone, where am I going?—

(you know)

—nowhere except away, left turn, left turn, right—

—right up the walk to the shelter, BROOKDALE and barking and Jake's truck, two other cars I don't recognize and here comes a girl and a guy, purple do-rag and Seahawks T-shirt, walking out with, yeah, the new slaphappy mutt between them: he's bouncing up and down and slobbering and choking himself with the leash, and they're smiling at each other and the dog and me, too, smiling all over like they just won the lottery and "Come on, Punkin," the girl says, tugging him gently toward the car. "Come on, baby, let's go home—"

—and all of a sudden I burst into tears, right there on the sidewalk like a little kid, a baby, I can't help it and I hate myself but I can't stop and "Oh hey," the girl says; she hands the leash to the guy. "Hey, what's wrong? Are you OK?"

No I'm not oh I'm so not but now she's digging in her bag for tissues, she's squeezing my shoulder, for some reason she thinks that the shelter's upset me and "It's not a sad place," she keeps saying. "My dad got his dog here, and we're getting Punkin— they're good people here, it's a good place. Really."

"I know," I say, or try to say—but do I know? A good place: how can I believe that anymore? Inside that building is a room with a steel table, the place where Grrl died alone, without me. How can that ever be a good place?

I wipe my eyes, my face, I see the mutt's face nosing the car window, leaving big smeary snuffle-prints: the girl laughs, and I smile too, you can't help smiling at something like that and "Get a dog," she says, patting my arm. "Really. . . . You going to be OK?"

"I'm OK." Wiping at my face. "Really."

She hops into the car, the mutt hops into her lap and she says something to me through the window, I can't hear her, they pull away and "Hey," another voice, close by, startling me: it's Karen, one of the volunteers, her purse on one arm and a bandage on the other and "You're back," she says, as if this is a good thing. She acts like she doesn't notice the bunched-up tissues, or my splotchy face. "How are you?"

"I'm OK," again, like it's all I know how to say; she looks at me, I look away and "I'm really sorry about the collie," she says, and I remember how she got that bandage: *she bit Karen.* It's a big bandage, a lot of gauze and tape. Big bandage for a bad bite. "It sucks, but it happens, you know?"

It happens: like the bandage on her arm, like a needle full of sleep, like me walking past the doors and down the grubby hall, into the smells and the barking, everything the same and not the same, never the same again . . . and here's the room, the table scratched and scoured by a thousand claws, paws, by Grrl's paws as she struggled, as she tried to get away, I'm crying again but I hardly feel it, feeling only the sense around me of, of vacuum, like the room's empty of everything, of pain and fear and even sadness, this room where Grrl's story came to an end, not the story I wrote but the story that is. The real story.

It sucks, but it happens.

And Grrl's the one it happened to, not me, even though you'd think I was the victim, even though the story I wrote—and all of a sudden I know this, like I've always known it, like my mind's finally snapped into focus here in this empty place—even *that* wasn't for Grrl, really, so much as it was for me. Not just because of the contest—though that *was* part of it, a little—but more like it was a story I was telling myself *about* myself, about me the big savior stepping in to help the poor dog, without seeing or wanting to see the real dog, the real Grrl, the beautiful furious damaged animal, damaged so deep that nothing I did was going to help her: no Wagalongs, no pen in the back yard, nothing but the hard kindness of the needle, to send her safely out of a world that had treated her so cruelly, a world that had ruined her, a world that to her was nothing but hunger and AFRAID.

And to be true to the real Grrl, the real story, I would have to show this room, that moment, where I should have been but wasn't and now could only go by writing about it, by showing others in words what it was like: for Grrl, for the people who were there, for all the people and animals who suffer. Because if I did that, and did it really well, then maybe—a tiny maybe, but a real one—maybe it wouldn't happen so much anymore. And maybe Grrl could be more than just her dying, more than just another sad stray dog.

The tissues are a soggy ball now, I really need to blow my nose: so out of the room and down the hall, into the bathroom, I want to leave before I see Melissa (or she sees me) but "Kiddo," and it's Jake with a big sad smile, he gives me a one-armed hug. "Wait a minute, I've got something for you."

He ducks into Melissa's office and comes back out with a plastic container, I know right away what it is and "Her ashes," he says. "I thought you might want to keep them."

"I do." The container is heavier than I thought it would be. Ashes. My beautiful Grrl. "Thanks, Jake."

"We'll miss you around here, you know," he says with that same sad smile. "Keeping us all on our toes. . . . I'll miss you."

"I'll miss you too." I can't cry any more, I'm all cried out, but if I could I would: because I will miss him, I'll miss being here, in these rooms with the dogs, working, helping, where will I go? but "Take care," I say, and turn, for the last time, for the door.

Outside the afternoon is glowing, budding trees and a deep mellow sun. I tuck Grrl's ashes into my backpack: I can feel them in there, like the ache in my heart, my special burden all the way home, all the way to my room where I set them carefully on the jumble of my dresser, right up front where I can see them. Then I drag my backpack onto the bed, make a space for myself in the nest of pillows, and open my notebook again.

AFRAID.

this place is all AFRAID, full of AFRAID like a storm cloud, a million buzzing bees, like hurt everywhere about to come and bite. i'm alone now with only They—one, two, many—who hold me down, hold me on strange high ground that no claws can dig into. in this high place i twist and growl, i struggle, oh! as hard as i can, but They are stronger, always stronger.

now They will hurt me. i know it.

why do They keep me here, the ones like me, the cats and all in boxes, caught, AFRAID? i want to be where there is no They, out on real ground dirt weeds sticks, ears up and listening to the wind, safe and running and—

—a bite! small and sharp in my leg, i feel it, feel something strange and cool where the teeth went in. *gooddog gooddog* They say, standing all around me. *gooddog.* is that like *straydog*?

the bite-hurt goes away fast; i feel the coolness everywhere now. i try to lift my head, to look around, but my head is heavy, my legs feel weak and soft, even on the ground i couldn't run. did the bite do that?

gooddog.

what's happening to me?

AFRAID AFRAID

afraid

as my eyes close, and open, and close again in the coolness like cool water, in the dark that comes to me like sleeping, a deep cool dark like

oh

11

"Griffin?" He's in his old seat, the window seat, not in the other desk by mine. Head to one side and his gaze is past me, like I'm not even there, a Lost Boy stare for sure but "Hey," I say; my voice sounds weird in my ears, like an echo chamber. I hate doing this here but I don't have a choice, I called him twice last night but he never called back. "I finished it, the dog thing. . . . Want to read it?"

He doesn't answer, his face is still as stone, a carved statue's face under the pale drift of his hair so "Here," I say, and leave it on the desk: wishing the room was empty, wishing I could talk to him alone, wishing he would at least look at me—but when I turn for my seat I see Mrs. Cruzelle looking at us both, something in her gaze I can't name, something sad. But she doesn't say anything, just starts up the class, *Macbeth* and line-reading and Griffin staring out the window like he's not even there at all.

Afterward I slog through Bio 2, Mr. Karpecky in his deadly lecture mode, I got lectured plenty at home yesterday but mostly it was just routine, stuff like *no one's angry, we were just worried, don't run off from school like that*. I didn't hear any grief from Mr. James or anybody so my mother must have called in to excuse me, I can just imagine what she said: *very distraught, a traumatic experience,* and so on and on. Which is true. I think—no, I know I've never cried so hard and so long, about anything. Even today, my eyes feel sore and dry, and I have a headache I can't get rid of.

At lunch, first thing I do is check the cafeteria, then the Media Center, then finally head alone for the steps. Sun dapples the parking lot, my Cappuccino Swirl is cool and sweet but all I can think of is Griffin: Did he read it? Will he read it? Is he ever going to talk to me again?

I wait all through lunch, but he never comes.

It's a long day, a long walk home, as soon as I get in the door I check for messages but there are none, or none for me anyway. I have a ton of homework—do these teachers even realize you have more than one class?—but I don't feel like doing it, I don't feel like doing anything, I don't know what to do with myself: no Grrl, no Griffin, no shelter, no essay, everything is over and done.

Eventually my mother comes in, front door bang, then cooking sounds from the kitchen: running water, the beep of the microwave and "Here," I say, stepping in, reaching past her for the carrot scraper. "I'll do that."

"Well, thank you," she says, eyebrows up, but at least she doesn't make a big thing about it, just steps aside and lets me work. It's soothing, somehow, to scrape at the carrots, make the little orange curls, something at least for my hands to do as my brain goes around and around.

After dinner the homework stares at me, I slog into it but my mind's not there, I keep making the same dumb mistakes over and over again, I have to do the Psych stuff twice. The TV drones from the living room; the phone rings—and tap-tap, "Rachel?" on my door, my heart gives a jump and "Phone for you," my mother says. It's Griffin, I know it is. Did he read the pages? Is he—

—but "Rachel?" a woman's voice, who is this? "It's Ruth Cruzelle."

Mrs. Cruzelle? and past the freefall of disappointment it feels weird, not only to talk to her outside of school but to talk to her like a person, one person calling another, I didn't even know her first name was Ruth. "Do you have a minute? I'm calling about your essay."

I won't ask you about it anymore: but she is; why? and "It's terrific," she says; she sounds really happy, like she just got a present she didn't expect to get. "Poignant and real and, and just terrific. I'm so pleased you decided to finish it."

"What?" I say, like an idiot, how did she—but "I've got a few suggestions, if you'd like to discuss them. You could stop in early tomorrow if you want."

"Mrs. Cruzelle, did you—did Griffin give you the pages?"

"He dropped them off after school, yes. —You know, it's enough that you wrote it, Rachel. You don't have to submit it to that essay contest, if you've changed your mind about—"

"No," I say, though I hadn't even thought about the contest when I was doing it: I just did it for Grrl. "No, that's OK. I can send it."

"Then I'll see you in the morning," and that's that, I put

down the phone and "I'm going out," I say to my mother, sitting at the kitchen table with a pile of files before her, a coffee in her hand. "I'll be back in a little while."

She doesn't ask where; does she know? "On the phone—that was your English teacher, right? the nice one? What did she have to say?"

"Good news," I say, shrugging into my jacket. "She told me good news."

A cool wind, not cold until I really get going, air streaming like water in my face, soothing my aching eyes. As I ride I pass through sounds like waves: thumping bass from someone's car, machine noise from a bright garage workshop, a barking dog's insistence, *Let me in.* Grrl never barked that way. All she wanted, ever could want, was out.

Oh God, I'm sorry, Grrl.

The lights are on inside his house, the car's in the driveway but at first no one hears me when I knock. But I keep trying, until finally "Hello," with one hand on the door, black sweater and calm gray eyes, no surprise at all to see me. "Griffin's upstairs—shall I call him?"

"I'll just go up, if that's OK."

As I pass her, Mrs. Gunn—Anna—touches my arm, lightly, briefly. "I was so sorry," she says, "to hear about the dog. Griffin's been quite upset; I'm sure you are too."

"I was. But I'm better now," and as I climb the stairs I know it's true. Not nearly good, not yet, but better, and maybe better still when— "Hey," startled, his hand on the door; he doesn't smile, but his face doesn't close up either, at least not all the way. Wary, like a shelter dog, peering out from the back of the cage, not sure how much to trust and "Mrs. Cruzelle called me," I say. I don't ask to come in, and he doesn't offer. "I just wanted to, to say thanks."

" 's OK." The way he says it makes me know that if things aren't all right again, at least they're not all wrong. "I thought she ought to read it—it was good."

Silence between us, but not the bad, cold kind: just a waiting kind. Then "You know," I say, "if you still want to, we can make the pen."

"Maybe. I don't know."

"How are you?" and before he can answer, "I'm five," I say. "Maybe five and a half, tops."

"I'm three," he says; he doesn't look at me. "Which is still better than yesterday. Yesterday was negative one."

"I'm sorry I yelled at you. None of this was your fault." I want to say more, but I know to wait: until later, until tomorrow at least so "I guess I'll see you at school," and I turn to go, down the stairs, I'm almost at the bottom when I hear—did I?—my name. I look back, the door's closed now . . . but still as I ride home I feel so much lighter, so much better, six for sure or maybe even seven: like things could go right again, like they did before; like we're back where we ought to be, Griffin and me.

Mrs. Cruzelle's working on her laptop and sipping coffee when I walk in; its scent fills the room, a warm dark hazelnut smell. When she sees me, she takes out my pages from the piles on her desk, reaches for her trusty red pencil and "I've made a few notes," she says, "a few things you might want to change, or expand. . . . And you definitely need to tell us what happens last. Not next, but last."

"I did." I shift off my backpack, let it slide, a slow thunk, onto my desk. "She—the dog dies."

She gives me one of those patented Mrs. Cruzelle looks, patient and sharp at the same time: "Are you sure that's the end?" but that's all she'll say about it, no hints or suggestions of what she's really thinking, what she wants me to do. Instead she starts talking about the contest, how I'll have to hustle to get the whole thing formatted right and mailed off before the deadline but "I know you can do it," she says. "If you can do *this*," tapping the pages, "you can do that."

Someone, a teacher I don't know, sticks his head in the doorway, sees me, and leaves. For some reason this strikes me as funny: *Danger, feral girl!* Mrs. Cruzelle sees my smile and smiles too, she's about to say something else but the bell goes, I reach for the pages and my backpack and "See you in class," she says.

Wading fast through the Walla-Wallas, I have to stop at my locker first, before Psych—and as I rush around the corner I smack right into someone, hard, "*Ow!*" and it's Chelsea Thayne, who glares at me like why in the world am I walking down *her* hall, why am I anywhere, "Watch where you're going!"

But you know what? I don't care. I'm not even mad, or, or anything, I just don't care. After what I've been through with Grrl, this girl is nothing, less than nothing, I don't even glare back at her because I don't have the time to waste so "Scuse me," I say, and step around her, on my way to where I have to be.

12

What happens last? Well, I don't know that yet, I mean as far as me and Griffin, and all the rest of it. But I can tell you what's happening now.

Let's see: it's summer, July and eighty-two degrees out here in Griffin's back yard. Sadie's drinking out of the concrete birdbath even though I've told her about a million times not to: "Sadie, stop," and here she comes, trying to jump up on my lap, wagging her tail like she's just pulled off the greatest trick ever known to dogdom and I must be just as happy about it as she is.

Sadie's part golden retriever, part Lab, part clown, and part who knows, her paws make stains on my Pet Depot T-shirt but that's OK. At a pet supply store, they expect a few muddy paws. In fact that's where we got her, Griffin and me: I went to drop off an application at Pet Depot, and that day they were having satellite adoptions, puppies and kittens and a few older animals, one of whom was Sadie: with her brown-and-white fur, and one bent ear, and her big sweeping tail that doesn't match the rest of her. The volunteer let her out of the crate, and she hopped around like she does, and climbed all over us, but when it was time to put her back she wouldn't go. Not like she was mean about it, or scared, or anything: she just *wouldn't go*, just kept looking at us with her big happy trusting eyes, until "I guess," Griffin said, "we have a dog."

We never did make the pen; Sadie didn't need it, she's a house dog. Anna—Griffin's mother—calls her the hair machine, but Anna's bed is where she sleeps at night.

Susan Jardine? No, I didn't go. I got the essay in on time, and I even got an honorable mention. But in the end she said it was "too raw," which kind of pissed off Mrs. Cruzelle, I think, but it made me smile. *Too raw*: just like Grrl. I told Mrs. Cruzelle not to worry about it, that I still had the key, and there are lots of other doors. Like that Young Authors thing they run at the library, maybe, or this other contest I read about online. . . . I sent a copy of the essay to Jake; he said he showed it to Melissa, but he didn't say what she thought of it. He also said I should take the summer off, and maybe come back to the shelter in the fall.

I don't know if I'll do that; I don't have to decide just yet. Right now I'm pretty happy at Pet Depot, getting people what they need to take care of their animals, helping out with the satellite adoptions—all my shelter experience comes in really handy there. Plus the money I make helps to pay off Brad for the computer, which he insisted I do; pay half, anyway. My mother says she considers the other half Brad's "donation," but I'm not sure what she means by that.

And when I'm not working, I'm writing: another story about a dog, part Sadie, part Grrl, part purely made-up. It's getting pretty long now, almost long enough for a book. Griffin wants me to send it to a publisher but *It's too raw*, I keep saying, though it really isn't, and he blows music at me through his horn. While I write, he plays; scales, notes up and down like stairsteps, again and again and again but with little variations each time. It's not really songs, but I like to listen to it anyway, especially out here, in the green cool of the yard, the leaves above us restless in the breeze.

I was the one who got him playing again, or practicing at least, which Anna says is a miracle. I don't know about that—it's not like he's going out for band or anything when we get back to school, but for now, he says, just playing is enough. I can't imagine Griffin in band anyway, unless they let him march the opposite way down the field.

Anna thinks we're "dating"; so does my mother. She calls Griffin my boyfriend, but I don't correct her anymore, except that "boyfriend" and "girlfriend" doesn't really describe what we are. I don't know if we need to describe it anyway; it's enough just to feel what it is.

Now it's almost time for work, I'm on for three to nine today. Griffin usually drives me, and Sadie rides in back, so I pick up her yellow leash and "Ride," I say, "Sadie, ride," and she immediately stops trying to crawl into my lap and starts hopping around, her tail going like a metronome, like a big brown beautiful broom, as "Ready?" through the screen door, Griffin in his Super Chicken T-shirt, keys in hand. "Let's go."

In the Pet Depot parking lot a woman pulls in next to us, a big gold-and-white dog in the car's back seat, a collie: tail swishing, eyes bright. Seeing her, my own eyes blur hot with tears, Griffin sees too and "You think," he says, "she's happy where she is now? Grrl, I mean?"

"She'd rather be alive," I say, when I can talk. "Alive and happy."

"Not the deal she got." He squeezes my hand. "See you after work, OK?"

Sadie tries to climb in Griffin's lap, then madly licks the back of my head. "OK," I say.

dark. i walk and sniff and wander through a strange clear darkness; i see others here, ones like me that walk on high hills, far away. when i get close i'll sniff and find out who they are.

my belly warm inside me, no hunger anymore, no thirst, did i have food? or water? i don't remember. wind against my fur as warm as sun, i trot on ground—grass, dirt, flowers—sniffing and looking, ears up and tail high: where am i? i don't know, don't care, not scared because there is no They here, no They smells, or cars, or boxes of lines that catch and hold . . . and most of all, best of all, no AFRAID, none. none! all gone, like a bad smell, like green water or cold rain, like a weight i carried always but no more. how can there be a place with no AFRAID? but there is. how did i get here? i don't know. just to be in this place, this warm and friendly dark, is good, and good enough.

i could stay here, always, and be glad. like the place so long ago, the small ones like me, the big one warm . . . maybe those ones are here too. even the big one. i know i can find them, if they are.

i go trotting deeper into clear kind darkness, ears up, toward the faraway. my tail goes back and forth, my legs are strong on the ground. soon i will be with the ones like me, all the straydogs, gooddogs, in the hills.